D1392949

Readers' Praise for *Fred-X Rising*

Student readers offer their thoughts

"This is a wonderful book and tons of people will enjoy it."

"You just want to keep reading on and on."

"It has a great story line and believable characters."

"I advise a sequel. It was very interesting. And hilarious."

"I liked the book. I liked how it flowed."

Adult readers react to Fred-X Rising

*"When is learning a foreign language fun?
When pigs fly! This book is a romp!"*

*"It made me laugh out loud at 6:00 in the morning all by myself,
and it made me long to go back to Italy one more time."*

*"The story is really darling and funny...a terrific way of learning
about one of my favorite countries and learning the language, too,
under very entertaining conditions."*

"A clever and engaging tale that makes you want to pack your bags and head for Italy—with your cat."

"If you like cats, airplanes, Italians and adventure, you'll love Fred-X Rising.*"*

"It shows you how learning another language also requires you to learn another culture; the two are inseparable."

"The approach to learning another language is fresh and original."

"I laughed out loud over and over. I love this book! The cats say things which we who are bound by political correctness would never be free to express."

I Gatti of the CIA:

FRED-X RISING

AVVENTURE IN ITALIA

George Arnold
From an oral account by
Dr. Buford Lewis, Ph.D.

Translations by Silvia Konrad
Illustrated by Jason C. Eckhardt

NORTEX PRESS  Austin, Texas

This book is a work of fiction, totally the creation of the author's imagination. Actual characters, organizations and locales are used only in a fictional context. Any similarity to real characters or events contained in this manuscript is purely coincidental.

Jason C. Eckhardt
ILLUSTRATOR
4 MEETINGHOUSE LANE
LITTLE COMPTON,
RHODE ISLAND · 02837
(401) 635-2762
·jeckhardt99@hotmail.com·

Typography by Pat Molenaar

FIRST EDITION
Copyright © 2006
By George Arnold
Manufactured in the U.S.A.
By Nortex Press
P.O. Drawer 90159 ⬯ Austin, Texas 78709-0159
ALL RIGHTS RESERVED.
1   2   3   4   5   6   7   8   9
ISBN 978-1-57168-898-9
ISBN 1-57168-898-6
Library of Congress Control Number 2006930681

For
Hannah, Mariel and Julianne—
their parents, aunts and uncle.
And other funny Italians all over the world

OTHER BOOKS BY GEORGE ARNOLD
From Sunbelt Media

Nonfiction

Growing Up Simple: An Irreverent Look at Kids in the 1950s

Foreword by Liz Carpenter. Winner of the IPPY Humor Award as the funniest book published in North America in 2003; the Violet Crown Award as the best nonfiction book by a Texas author in 2003; and a coveted TPRA Silver Spur.

BestSeller: Must-Read Author's Guide to Successfully Selling Your Book

Published authors and writers who want to be published learn how to avoid rejection and end up selling their manuscripts and five, ten, twenty times as many of their published books.

Fiction

Los Gatos of the CIA: Hunt for Fred-X

Foreword by Frank Devlyn, Mexico City. The four Texan cats—los cuatro gatos tejanos—and their sidekick Cincinnati the dancing pig go to Mexico in search of the infamous Fred-X, giant spotted owl who's stealing todos los gatos méjicanos (all the cats of Mexico), flying them to the Yucatán and selling them into slavery in Aruba. A funny adventure for juvenile readers and, for adults, a tongue firmly-in-cheek spoof on the Tom Clancy, Robert Ludlum, Clive Cussler spy adventure genre. Complete with 750 words and phrases in Spanish.

New Nonfiction—Coming Soon

Chick Magnates, Televangelist Imams, A Pig Farmer's Beef

Hilarious, but true, tales from the world of advertising agencies—those creative people who cause you to just have to have stuff you don't really need and buy things you can't really afford.

Spencer & Bennett —

Non dimenticare che i gatti sono molto abili.

I Gatti of the CIA:

FRED-X RISING

AVVENTURE IN ITALIA

George Arnold

www.CIAcats.com

* Contents *

* Cast of Characters *

Luisa Manicotti Giaccomazza*—Wise, thoughtful and seriously funny little orange tabby twin to Luigi.

Césare Pepperoni Giaccomazza—Jaunty gray tabby cousin of Luigi and Luisa. Head of the Rome Bureau of Interpol. Reputed to be a serious crime-fighter. His ever-present yellow straw fedora and his moon-walking rapper gait mask his more serious side.

Poinsettia Fiore DeVille—Interpol lieutenant and first assistant to Césare. Known to her friends and fellow agents as *Tenente Poni*. A stunningly gorgeous calico with enormously long eyelashes and a no-nonsense demeanor that keeps her boss focused.

Supporting Cast

Fred-X—Giant spotted owl. International rogue known most recently for stealing cats in Mexico, flying them to the Yucatán and selling them into slavery in Aruba. Just escaped from the custody of the Federales in Mexico after being tracked down and jailed by Buzzer, Cincinnati and friends.

Frieda K—Fred-X's girlfriend. A European owl of unknown intentions, but no criminal record. Yet.

Cameo Appearances by

Il Papa—His eminence, the Pope.

Dr. Buford Lewis, Ph.D.*—Manager of Buzzer's little ranch in the Texas hill country. The only living Labrador retriever with a doctor of philosophy degree. Professor *emeritus* and holder of the Rin Tin Tin Chair of Literature at the University of California at Barkley. Former press secretary to a succession of governors of California.

* x *

Bogart-BOGART*—Buford's brother and assistant ranch manager. Often lost in deep thought, Bogart-BOGART is extremely smart—a real thinker.

Signor Mano di Legno—Employee of the *municipio* of Moena in charge of taking care of the village hall's two cats, making deliveries and other odd jobs.

Cardinal Umberto Uccello—Vatican resident and close advisor to *il Papa*—the Pope. The good cardinal may have turned from a life of religious devotion to the worldly pursuit of megabucks. Birds of a feather do flock together.

Dominus and Vobiscum—Undercover crows working secretly for the Swiss Guard at the Vatican to expose a crooked, blackmailing cardinal.

Demos—Solid black Greek cat. Leader of a troupe of motorcycle-riding stunt cats who travel the world putting on daredevil shows of amazing feats on wheels.

---

*Real, live animals who actually do live together in the Texas hill country.

* Prologue *
I Gatti (the Cats)
of the CIA

Buzzer Louis and Cincinnati the dancing pig's first adventure after retiring from the CIA (Cats In Action, a secret international crime-fighting team run out of the White House basement by Socks, Chelsea Clinton's house pet) involved the banishment of that evil cat-stealing rogue Fred-X from the U.S.

You see, in his job as a parcel delivery bird, Fred-X had busied himself on the side by stealing cats and flying them to Memphis every night. To be sold into the international slave trade. Buzzer and Cincinnati, though, were just too clever for poor old Fred-X. A week-long game of cat-and-owl began in the hills of Texas and ended up in Ohio. Buzzer and Cincinnati brought the giant spotted owl to his wingtips. They banished him to South America with the promise never to steal another cat.

Two years later, *el presidente* Vicente Fox of *Méjico* had called on Buzzer and Cincinnati to come to his country to help the *federales*, Mexican national police, capture the shady Fred-X. Seems the busy but somewhat dimwitted owl had once again begun to steal cats—this time Mexican cats, whom he flew nightly to the *Yucatán* to be sold into slavery in Aruba. Buzzer and Cincinnati, with Buzz's sister Dusty as their Spanish-speaking interpreter, and their tiny twin siblings Luigi and Luisa along for comic relief, helped the *federales* track Fred-X from *Chihuahua* to *Mérida* on the *Yucatán* peninsula. There, in a clever plot hatched by Buzzer, Cincinnati and *la cucaracha*, the *curandera* (medicine woman) of the *Primos* Indian tribe, our international crime fighters captured Fred-X and his meek *complíce* (accomplice), *señor Tal Vez*. They turned the evil pair over to the *federales*, who promptly popped them *en carcél*—into jail.

In Mexico city, Buzzer, Cincinnati, Dusty, Luigi and Luisa were hailed as national heroes and presented with beautiful medals and a one million peso reward by *el presidente* Fox, himself, as the world watched on CNN.

Barely a week after returning to their little ranch in the quiet Texas hill country, our crime-fighting heroes learned that Fred-X had escaped from Mexican jail and was reported to be flying under his own power to Rome, where his girlfriend Frieda-K would meet him.

The phone rang once again at the little ranch. This time the call was from Italy. From Luigi and Luisa's cousin, Césare Pepperoni Giaccomazza. Césare, you see, is bureau chief of the Rome office of Interpol, international law enforcement agency.

And so, the newest adventure of *Los Gatos* (now *I Gatti*) of *the CIA* begins.

Brief Author's Note

Vowels and vowel combinations are pronounced differently in Italian than in English. As you read along and encounter Italian words, if you want to know how to say them, you'll find them in the glossary and pronunciation guide at the end of the book.

Part One

Back in Action

"We've tracked down Fred-X twice already, only to
have him escape from someone else's custody.
Maybe this time will be the charm."

—Buzzer Louis
Retired DO/CIA

* Chapter 1 *
The Euro Bureau Calls

"Allora, ciao, Césare."[1]

Luigi Panettone Giaccomazza clicked off the phone and looked up, smiling. The tiny orange tabby kitten knew something nobody else in the room knew. And he couldn't wait for someone to ask him about it.

"Who was it, Luigi?" His tiny twin sister, Luisa Manicotti Giaccomazza, asked the question first.

"That was our cousin Césare Pepperoni Giaccomazza in Rome." Luigi answered the question his sister had asked, but offered no further information.

"Well?" Luisa persisted.

"Well, what?" Luigi responded. He was going to make someone ask the question everyone wanted the answer to.

"Luigi, don't be difficult," their older brother Buzzer Louis, a black-and-white tuxedo cat, stepped into the questioning. "You know what we all want to know. Spit it out, Luigi."

---

1. "Goodbye, then, Césare." Ciao is also used as a greeting, to say "hello."

"OK, sorry, Buzzer." Luigi wasn't really all that sorry, but he knew it was time to stop playing games and get on with the story. "Césare's the agent-in-charge of the Rome station of Interpol."

He stopped talking again, looking around at the assembled faces staring at him and waiting. He could tell Luisa was willing to wait him out. She knew his tricks, and she wouldn't fall for them. Not one of them. His big brother Buzzer Louis and older sister Dusty Louise, a pretty gray tabby, were used to his games, too. He knew he could string them out a bit longer before Dusty Louise lost her patience and simply exploded. The joker in Luigi's deck, though, was Buzzer Louis' friend and former sidekick in the CIA, Cincinnati the dancing pig.

"How far can I push Cincinnati?" Luigi wondered silently, thinking to himself that maybe, just maybe, he had strung out the suspense long enough. Maybe he had better get on with telling everyone gathered in the great room of the Texas hill country ranch house what the phone call from Italy had *really* been all about. "Cincinnati may crack first. And I don't want him mad at me. At least not right now," he thought to himself.

Luigi's brain raced.

He decided to speak. To dole out a little more. And then measure the tension once again.

"Mio cugino Césare[2] said Fred-X has landed near the Vatican. He's in Rome, and it looks like he's just waiting for his girlfriend to contact him. Césare says the Interpol station in Munich reports she's headed south toward Rome from Germany. Her name's Frieda-K."

---

2. My cousin Césare.

Luigi smiled. He looked and felt relieved. He had spit out everything he really knew just before someone, likely Cincinnati, had completely lost patience with him. In Luigi's world, that meant he had won.

"Chalk up another small win for the Luigi-ster," he thought to himself proudly.

"So, Luigi, what does Interpol want us to do?" Buzzer asked with an edge to his voice that told Luigi the game was over. *Finito*.[3] Buzz guessed the group was about to get involved in owl-hunting. And soon. After all, he and Cincinnati are the world's foremost experts on the evil ways of Fred-X.

"Do we need to go to Rome?" Buzz pushed on. To be sure Luigi understood he wanted some answers. And he wanted them now.

Seeing Buzz's patience with his little game was over, Luigi got serious. Being serious, ever, was not an easy thing for the little kitten to do. But one that was clearly necessary.

"Césare has an Interpol team watching Fred-X right now. He thinks the owl's too tired to cause much mischief right away," Luigi said. "Of course, he's just spent several days flying all the way from the Yucatán to Italy. That's a long haul without an airplane," Luigi continued, adding as only Luigi could in his own peculiar form of jump-speak, "not to mention there's no place to rest along the way."

"We could leave here in the morning and be there in eight or nine hours." It was Cincinnati the dancing pig, ignoring Luigi's strange, disconnected speaking style and offering his own opinion. And his new airplane, *The Flying Pig Machine*.

---

3. Finished.

Specially equipped for long-range flight. With himself as captain and chief pilot, of course. "My plane's just sitting out at the Hill Country Intergalactic Airport, all fueled up and ready to go. Dusty can be my co-pilot."

Cincinnati sounded almost smitten with wanderlust. Or at least with a burning desire to do in that evil owl Fred-X once and for all. And quickly.

Dusty had started to learn to fly on their trip last week to Mexico, exchanging Spanish lessons with Cincinnati in return for flying lessons. Forgetting her impatience with Luigi's little game, she fairly beamed at the chance to once again help fly Cincinnati's beautiful new Sabreliner. And on a long, transAtlantic flight this time.

Buzzer Louis, normally thoughtful and slow to react, turned to Luigi and commanded him, "Call Césare back. Tell him we'll be leaving here tomorrow at daybreak. Hmmm, let's see. With the seven-hour time difference and nine hours to get there, we'll be in Rome by about 10 P.M. tomorrow night.

"Ask him to keep a close eye on that crazy owl. Don't let him get away again."

"Yahoo!" The squeaky chorus resounded. Luigi and Luisa, freshly rested from their Mexican adventure, were ready like kittens everywhere to hit the road yet again.

"This time we'll be the interpreters," Luisa said, looking straight at Dusty Louise as if to say, "You're not the only cat who can speak two languages." Dusty's knowledge of Spanish had been very helpful in Mexico, but now they were going to Italy. And like kittens everywhere, Luigi and Luisa were born speaking Italian. And still young enough to remember it all.

"You be the interpreter, Luisa," Luigi said quickly. "I'll probably be way too busy being *il segugio di prim'ordine*."[4]

"*Sicuro. Senza dubbio!*[5] Luigi." Luisa laughed at her twin brother's bravado, then smiled sweetly to let him know she wasn't making fun of him. "You'll be a great, great *segugio*, Luigi," she added, looking directly at Dusty who was pouting because she didn't understand the exchange.

Reassured, Luigi grabbed his little yellow *valigetta*[6]. Luisa ran for her red one. They were on the job and ready to go. Both were packed this time. Just in case.

Cincinnati sat down at the long dining room table. He opened his pilot's sample case and pulled out a laptop computer, some maps, a protractor and two small plastic triangles. "We'll go from here to Gander, Newfoundland," he said. "We'll gas up there and make a straight run into Rome. The polar or maybe the great circle route will be fastest. Luigi, get on that phone to Césare," Cincinnati reminded the little kitten. "Tell him 9 P.M. in Rome. This pilot pig can cut at least an hour off Buzz's schedule. And we won't even have to rush."

While Cincinnati was plotting a course, checking worldwide flying weather at ADDS on the internet and pulling together a flight plan, Buzzer slipped quietly outside to find Dr. Buford Lewis, Ph.D., and Buford's very smart younger brother, Bogart-BOGART. Buzz needed to tell them about the upcoming trip. And to retrieve a pair of little satellite phones the two brothers had "borrowed" when Buzzer came back from Mexico last week. Buzzer had never quite understood why the

---

4. the super sleuth
5. "Sure. No doubt."
6. Small suitcase, or valise.

two Labrador retrievers wanted to call one another from opposite sides of the barn, anyway.

"It must be a dog-thing," he thought to himself.

Back in the house, Luigi was winding up a short return phone call to Césare.

"Allora, mio cugino. Domani alle ventuno a Fiumicino."[7]

"An Interpol team will meet us at Fiumicino, the big airport in Rome at about twenty-one hundred tomorrow night. That's nine o'clock in Rome, right?" Luigi asked nobody in particular.

"Right you are, Luigi," Luisa answered, thinking to herself that only those who understood Italian could also possibly be on top of the workings of a twenty-four hour clock.

Luigi continued his report on the call. "Césare said to taxi to the Jet-Sweep private plane terminal. There's a meeting room there where we can meet with Interpol and plot and plan." Luigi put on his most mysterious-looking face.

Buzzer, walking into the room holding the two satellite phones and chargers, caught the end of Luigi's report and added, "Plot and plan is right, Luigi. Probably more 'plot' than 'plan.' Thanks for setting it up for us."

"Sí, sí mio fratello,"[8] Luigi responded, standing up tall and saluting Buzzer while looking at Dusty to see if she understood what he was saying. She was frowning again, which secretly pleased Luigi and Luisa. Dusty had been, shall we say, somewhat less than nice on their trip to Mexico when occasionally the little kittens didn't understand what she was saying in Spanish.

---

7. "Then until 9 P.M. tomorrow night, cousin, at *Fiumicino* (Rome's airport)."
8. "Yes, yes, my brother."

"Serves her right," Luisa whispered to Luigi with a sly smile.

Cincinnati and Dusty, the flight crew for Cincinnati's sleek new twin-fanjet Sabreliner, were still at the dining room table poring over charts and maps and trying to figure out the best way to avoid an arctic cold front that was making its way quickly across Quebec. When Buzzer came back into the room, Cincinnati looked up and called to him, "Buzz, we could use some help here. C'mon over and help us unpuzzle this riddle." He pointed to a big map spread out on the table. The Great Lakes were in the middle of it. "We can go north and around. Or we can go south and around. But I don't want to go through this front. It tops out above 50,000 feet. And it's full of ice."

Buzzer sat down beside Cincinnati and Dusty, surrounded by their menagerie of laptop computers, charts, maps, triangles, protractors and assorted mysterious stuff. The three of them began to point, mumble, shake their heads and generally look like a boring, not-very-fun group to Luigi and Luisa, who were poking some last-minute snacks into their little suitcases. "Just in case Cincinnati forgot to order any goodies for the galley on *The Flying Pig Machine*," Luisa assured nobody in particular.

"Buzz said we're leaving at daybreak. The Mini-Mart won't be open in time for us to stock up on the way to the airport," she smiled at Luigi who agreed with her completely. No need to risk hunger pangs on the way to see the polar bears at Mother Gooseland. Or wherever it was Cincinnati had said they would stop to refuel. "He said something about polar bears and geese. Or a goose. I remember that much." Luisa turned to Luigi, a puzzled look on her face.

Luigi couldn't remember exactly, either.

"I wish we could stop for a few hours in Mother Gooseland and see the polar bears, Luigi. That might be fun," Luisa looked wistful.

"Are you sure he said Mother Gooseland, Luisa? I wasn't paying attention," Luigi admitted quietly. And only to his little twin, his closest friend in the world.

"Of course you weren't paying attention, Luigi. You were just trying to see how long you could keep from reporting on your phone call with Césare before Dusty blew her stack," Luisa said. "I was kind of hoping you would wait just a tad bit more. She was getting puffy cheeks and her eyes were just starting to twitch. Another ten seconds and, wow, she would have gone off like Mount Vesuvius. Hey, that's close to Rome, isn't it? Maybe if we can't stop long enough to meet some polar bears at Mother Gooseland, we could go to the old volcano. Whaddaya think, Luigi?"

"I don't know, Luisa. Once Buzzer and Cincinnati get on the trail of that Fred-X bird, they kind of lose their sense of having fun. Know what I mean?" Luigi asked. "Maybe we could just disappear for a while at Mother Gooseland. They would have to wait for us to come back to the plane, wouldn't they?"

"Or they might just leave us there. Dusty would," Luisa thought out loud. "That might not be so bad except if it really isn't Mother Gooseland. It could be a terrible place, you know. I wish I could remember for sure what Cincinnati said."

While the two kittens tried to remember exactly where

Cincinnati had said they would stop to refuel, the dancing pig, Dusty, and Buzzer Louis were solving the riddle of getting around the cold front racing across Canada. They would get the plane into Gander, Newfoundland, to refuel on their way to Rome, missing the ice-filled weather front along the way.

"If we can get away from here by about 5:30 in the morning, we can set a course over Cleveland and on to Bangor, Maine. Then north to Gander," Cincinnati was saying. "We can be there in less than four hours, refuel and head to Rome at least ninety minutes ahead of the weather. I'm sure glad I got that long-range pack for my plane. Let's just get everybody to bed early so we can get off the ground at daybreak." He looked to Buzzer and Dusty for agreement, shook his head 'yes' and started folding up his maps and charts, making a few notes to plug into the onboard computer on *The Flying Pig Machine* in the morning.

Buzzer turned to where Luigi and Luisa were quietly thinking about their chances of abandoning ship for a few hours of fun with the polar bears in Mother Gooseland. He spoke directly to them. "Listen up, you two. We're leaving early in the morning. So off to bed with you. You need to be ready and rested. Remember, early to bed and early to rise . . ."

". . . will give you a headache and bloodshot eyes." Luigi finished Buzzer's sentence and he and Luisa burst into raucous laughter.

"That was pretty funny, Luigi," Buzzer admitted. "But we all need to get to bed and get some shuteye. Tomorrow is going to be a long, long day. And we have our work cut out for us in re-capturing Fred-X. Let's not forget our real mission. Keep your eyes on the rabbit."

"What rabbit⸮" Luisa whispered to Luigi. Is there going to be a rabbit in Rome⸮ Or in Mother Gooseland⸮ What's Buzzer talking about⸮"

"I don't know, either, Luisa. Maybe he's losing it. Let's just play along and pretend we're looking at a rabbit," Luigi offered. "If that'll make him happy, let's just do it."

"I think what'll make him happy is for us to go to bed, Luigi. Let's just get going. You pretend you're watching that rabbit and just follow me. *Buona notte, fratello mio.*"[9]

As the tiny twin tabbies head off to bed, what do you think they'll dream about⸮ Polar bears⸮ Mother Gooseland⸮ Invisible rabbits⸮ And what of Cincinnati and Dusty⸮ They have a long way to fly Cincinnati's plane tomorrow. Will they get enough sleep to stay awake all the way to Rome⸮ And what about Césare⸮ Is he really the agent-in-charge of the Interpol office in Rome⸮ Will he and his fellow agents be able to keep Fred-X in one place until Buzzer and friends arrive tomorrow night⸮ Will Frieda-K get there first⸮

---

9. Good night, brother.

Impariamo un po' d'Italiano.

(We're Going to Learn a Little Italian.)

By Luisa Manicotti Giaccomazza

If you ever go to Rome like we're about to do,
you will want to be able to speak a little Italian.

In English	In Italian	Say It Like This
COUNTING TO TEN		
one	*uno*	OO-noh
two	*due*	DOO-eh
three	*tre*	tray
four	*quattro*	KWAT-troh
five	*cinque*	CHEEN-kway
six	*sei*	say
seven	*sette*	SET-teh
eight	*otto*	OH-toh
nine	*nove*	NOH-veh
ten	*dieci*	dee-AY-chee
SOME COMMON COLORS		
red	*rosso*	ROH-soh
blue	*azurro*	ah-ZOO-roh
white	*bianco*	bee-AHN-coh
green	*verde*	VAIR-deh
yellow	*giallo*	JAHL-loh
black	*nero*	NAIR-oh
gold	*oro*	OHR-oh
gray	*grigio*	GREE-joh
orange	*arancione*	ah-rahn-CHOH-neh

* Chapter 2 *
Andiamo a Roma[1]

The Vatican—Near Rome, Italy

"*Allora*,[2] Poni, he's still lying there. Right in the same place."

Césare Pepperoni Giaccomazza, bureau chief of the Rome office of Interpol, pulled the binoculars from his eyes and set them down on a ledge. He tugged down the brim of his jaunty yellow straw fedora to shade his eyes from the pink glow of the rising sun.

He and his assistant, Lieutenant Poinsettia Fiore DeVille, had spent the entire night watching Fred-X, who was apparently sleeping in the corner of the piazza[3] under a bush near the Vatican radio station.

"He must be pretty tired if he flew all the way from the Yucatán to Rome," Poinsettia responded. The lieutenant was a gorgeous calico cat with long, tapering eyelashes that set off

---

1. Let's go to Rome.
2. now then
3. plaza, square

her yellow eyes and made them look as big as saucers. Everyone called her *Tenente*[4] Poni.

The gray tabby Césare handed the binoculars to Poni and glanced around at the rooftops. He had three additional two-cat teams watching the evil Fred-X. They were all there. Eight of them, all night long. Watching a giant bird who looked to be sleeping.

As he remembered their long, chilly vigil, another thought popped through his head. "You don't suppose he's dead, do you, Poni?"

Poni trained the binoculars on the big bird, adjusted the focus and squinted ever so slightly to get a better look. "No, not dead. I can see his chest rising and falling. And his mouth opens and closes very slightly. He sure looks like he's breathing to me."

Then she changed the subject as only women are allowed to do. "When are these *cugini*[5] of yours from *gli Stati Uniti*[6]

---

4. lieutenant
5. cousins
6. United States

going to show up, Césare? And what do they care about this stupid bird, anyway?"

"We're expecting them at *Fiumicino*[7] at about twenty-one hundred hours tonight, Poni. They captured Fred-X in Mexico ten days ago only to have him escape from jail. Remember, Buzzer Louis and Cincinnati the dancing pig know more about the ways of Fred-X than anybody. That's why I called them for help."

"Why don't we just go on down there and arrest him?" Poni asked.

"Two reasons, *tenente*. We're waiting for a fugitive warrant from Mexico. He hasn't done anything illegal yet in Italy. At least, nothing that we know about. Besides, he's in the Vatican. Italian police, including us as long as we're operating here, can't arrest anyone in the Vatican. So we can't just go grab him, much as I'd like to do just that."

"Do you know this Buzzer Louis and the dancing pig Cincinnati, Césare?" Poinsettia asked. "How do they know so much about Fred-X?"

"Do I know them? Yes, you bet I do. They once saved the life of *Il Papa*[8] right in this very *piazza*. I was here within minutes after they foiled a Middle Eastern assassin. He was trying to plant plastic explosives in the popemobile. What a job they did that night!

"And I was with them four years ago in North Africa. Wait 'til you hear this. *Mamma mia!*[9] They are truly geniuses for

---

7. Name of the big airport in Rome
8. The Pope.
9. Literally, "Mother of mine!" More accurately translated as "Goodness gracious."

sure." Césare pushed back the brim of his yellow straw hat and rolled his eyes up as if he were about to become totally lost in thought.

"Tell me about it, Césare," Tenente Poni asked. "What happened?"

Césare stared off into the bloom of the early morning sun as it peeped over the hills of Rome. "You keep those binoculars on Fred-X, Poni, and I'll tell you all about Africa.

"We were trailing the East German executioner, Erwin the Weasel. Remember him?"

"Oh, sure. How could anyone forget Erwin?" Poni answered, keeping the binoculars trained on the corner of the *piazza*.

"*Allora*, Cincinnati had picked up Erwin's scent as the vermin left Antwerp and was headed, so we thought, for Addis Ababa. He was on his way to assassinate Ethiopia's world-champion long distance runner, Ahmad the Stick. But like all criminals, Erwin made a simple mistake. He reserved a Land Rover in Egypt at Avis. Buzzer's bosses at Cats in Action zeroed in on that reservation instantly.

"Buzz and Cincinnati joined me here in Rome and we took one of Interpol's fast Bell Jet Ranger helicopters straight across the Mediterranean to Alexandria. But by the time we got there, Erwin the Weasel had picked up his desert car and had about a two-hour head start on us. We came upon his tracks somewhere near the southern Egyptian border. In no time we had the British Racing Green Land Rover in our sights. But how to capture him? We knew he had two of his *capo dei capi*[10]

---

10. first assistants, or leaders, usually criminal "enforcers."

with him. And you can bet they had plenty of firepower in that Land Rover. Their usual arsenal of Kalishnikovs, for sure. And probably some small missiles, too."

"What did you do, Césare? How could you take on those kinds of weapons?" Poni wrinkled her brow but kept the binoculars tight to her eyes and trained on the sleeping Fred-X.

"Well, *tenente*, while I was still thinking about what might be a bloody confrontation, Buzzer Louis spoke the obvious. 'We don't want to take them head on,' he said. 'That would be really stupid. But here's a way to get them.' And in thirty seconds, Buzzer and Cincinnati the dancing pig had planned a capture so diabolical it just had to work. And, of course, it did."

Césare paused and looked at Poni. He had the same mischievous time-delay genes as his little cousin Luigi Panettone Giaccomazza.

"Stop playing games, Césare. You know that makes me mad enough to challenge a pit bull to thumb wrestle. And cats don't even have thumbs. Now what was the diabolical plan and how did it work?" The pretty *tenente* suddenly became stern, a tactic she had learned was needed from time to time to keep her boss in line.

Césare pretended to be chastised but he and the lieutenant both knew it was an act.

"We raced ahead of the Land Rover about twenty kilometers. We hid our helicopter behind a big sand dune and set up a roadside barbecue sandwich stand. Cincinnati printed a sign in German that said *Delicious Pork Barbecue Sandwiches—Only Five Euros*. We put that sign on a stick and pounded it into the sand beside the road. Then we strapped a long pole to Cincinnati's back and hung him over a little pit—as if he were a pig being roasted on a spit. Our helicopter pilot sat beside a makeshift counter and pretended to be a desert barbecue baron. Buzzer and I hid out of sight and waited for the Land Rover to stop."

"Very clever setup, Césare. Staging a trap is one thing. But pulling it off is quite another. How'd you do that?" *Tenente* Poinsettia Fiore DeVille was getting a bit anxious to get to the big finish with somewhat less along-the-way storytelling.

"Well, Poni, this little oasis was the only stopping place for a hundred kilometers in any direction. We had some sausages and bread in the helicopter. We'd brought them along for an afternoon snack. Buzz laced them with just enough knockout drops to help us subdue Erwin the Weasel and his *due capi*[11].

---

11. two assistants.

They stopped just like we knew they would. Got out and demanded barbecue sandwiches while they held Kalishnikov automatics on our poor pilot. He handed them three of the makeshift sandwiches laced with knockout drops. They began to gobble. Cincinnati was turning slowly on the spit over the pit with no fire in it. Suddenly he leaped down, grabbed the stick that was attached to his back and rushed Erwin and his cohorts. Cincinnati screamed. 'Weasel steak on Texas toast, please' to the pilot-turned-barbecue-stand attendant. He made such a commotion so quickly that Erwin and his fellow assassins froze. Buzz and I simply walked up behind them, gave them the old back o' the knee shove and—in an instant—had them all in cuffs.

"Neat and tidy. And quick."

"Wow!" *Tenente* Poni was impressed. But if she seemed speechless, it wasn't from the recounting of Cincinnati's derring-do. No, it was because she suddenly saw something big coming toward them in the morning sky.

✳   ✳   ✳

Gander, Newfoundland

"Gander tower, this is Sabreliner seven zero niner niner alpha. We're twenty-five miles southwest on direct requesting permission to land and refuel." Dusty Louise, in the co-pilot's seat with headphones clipped snugly over her ears, spoke into her microphone.

"Sabreliner seven zero niner niner, Gander tower here. You are cleared to land. Taxi directly to the Chevron sign for refueling. And welcome to Newfoundland, miss."

It was midmorning. As planned, the little group of owl-catchers had left the Hill Country Intergalactic Airport just before dawn. Cincinnati the dancing pig was in the pilot's seat and Dusty Louise was right up front beside him.

"That's it! New Fun Land, Luisa." Luigi's eyes lit up like sparklers. "Gander must be Mother Goose's husband, you think?"

"Or her brother, maybe," Luisa answered. She glanced over to Buzzer, who was staring out the window by his left shoulder. "Buzzy, can we stay and play awhile here in New Fun Land? Can we go see Mother Goose?" Luisa was pleading as only Luisa could do.

Luigi joined the begging. "Yes, Buzzer, can't we stop for just a little while. I want to ride the roller coaster. I love roller coasters. They're really fun. Up, down, around the corner. Back up again. Can we, Buzzy? Pleeez?" Luigi concluded by throwing both front paws up and out as if to be ready to catch a "yes" answer tossed back to him by his big brother.

"What are you two talking about?" Buzzer Louis looked puzzled, but amused at the twin tabbies' questioning.

"About New Fun Land," Luigi piped right up. "Is it an amusement park, Buzzy?"

"Isn't this where Mother Goose lives?" Luisa wanted to know for sure.

Before Buzzer could answer, the sleek jet's tires touched down on the concrete runway with a screech. Cincinnati reversed the fanjets' thrusters and hit the brakes, bringing the little jet from a 160 miles per hour to taxi speed in just a few seconds.

"We're on the ground, Cincinnati," Dusty Louise said. "Can I take the controls now?"

"You have the stick, Dusty." Cincinnati leaned back. He raised his front legs up high and stretched his lower back muscles. "Take us to the Chevron sign over there."

While Dusty Louise was taxiing *The Flying Pig Machine* to the Chevron pumps to refill its tanks, Buzzer was trying to unscramble the tiny kittens' confused notions about where they had landed.

"This is Gander, Luigi and Luisa. Gander's the name of a city in Newfoundland. Gander has nothing to do with geese. Or Mother Goose. I'm sorry if you're disappointed. The country is Newfoundland. Like New Found Land. It's one of the most eastern points in North America. And it's a good place to stop to fill up our tanks before we head across the North Atlantic Ocean. There's not an amusement park here. Sorry."

"Are you sure, Buzzer? Are you really, *really* sure?" Luisa was not one to give up her notions easily. Even if they were somewhat off base.

Luigi joined in the questioning. "Have you been here before, Buzzer? I mean, have you scouted around for roller coasters and other fun stuff?"

"I've stopped here before, yes. But just to refuel. I guess I've never left the airport." Buzzer smiled at the little twins.

"There! That proves it! You just didn't know that Mother Goose lives here and there's a giant roller coaster right down the road. Can we go, Buzzy? Please?" Luigi tried some big cat slam-dunk logic.

"Not this morning, guys. Remember we have to hurry to Rome to help Césare and his Interpol team wrap up that evil owl Fred-X. Maybe on the way back we can take a cab and look around a bit. If Mother Goose really lives here, we might just find her," Buzzer smiled at the innocence and imaginations of his baby kitten brother and sister. "I can't remember ever being that young and excited," he thought to himself.

"Everybody out for a stretch." Captain Cincinnati pulled a handle to open the front door and lower the stairs. "Walk around and get your blood pumping again. But don't go far. We'll want to get going again pretty quickly."

With that, he bounded down the stairs, doing a perfect *pas de deux* as he stepped lightly onto the tarmac. Cincinnati looked up and smiled. He knew not even his cat friends could do what he'd just done. He was a dancer to be sure. And quite an athlete.

What do you think *Tenente* Poni saw coming toward her and Césare in Rome's morning sky? Does Mother Goose really live in Gander? At an amusement park with a big roller coaster? And what of Fred-X? Is he going to sleep until our crime fighters from *gli Stati Uniti* get to Rome?

Impariamo un po' d'Italiano.

(We're Going to Learn a Little Italian.)

By Luisa Manicotti Giaccomazza

In English	In Italian	Say It Like This
DAYS OF THE WEEK		
Sunday	domenica	doh-MIN-ee-cah
Monday	lunedí	loo-neh-DEE
Tuesday	martedí	mahr-teh-DEE
Wednesday	mercoledí	mair-coh-leh-DEE
Thursday	giovedí	joh-veh-DEE
Friday	venerdí	ven-ehr-DEE
Saturday	sabato	SAH-bah-toh
MONTHS OF THE YEAR		
January	gennaio	jin-NY-yo
February	febbraio	fehb-BRY-oh
March	marzo	MAHR-zoh
April	aprile	ah-PREE-lay
May	maggio	MAH-joe
June	giugnio	JOO-nyo
July	luglio	LOO-lyo
August	agosto	ah-GOH-stoh
September	settembre	set-TEHM-bray
October	ottobre	oht-TOH-bray
November	novembre	noh-VEHM-bray
December	dicembre	dee-CHIM-bray

* Chapter 3 *
Césare–Un Gatto Preoccupato[1]

The Vatican—within Rome

"*E` un gufo smisurato, Césare!*"[2]

Tenente Poni pulled the binoculars from her eyes and turned to talk directly to her boss at Interpol, Césare Pepperoni Giaccomazza. "It's a giant owl, and it's headed straight for the *piazza*," she added.

"Must be the girlfriend, Frieda-K, Poni," Césare answered. He picked up his tiny two-way radio and clicked the transmit button. "*Quí é il direttore.*"[3] He spoke into the microphone to alert the other three two-cat teams watching Fred-X on the stakeout. "Looks like the girlfriend's approaching at eleven o'clock about thirty degrees off the horizon. Let's get the rotors on the *elicottero*[4] turning. Just in case they take off

---

1. Césare—One Worried Cat
2. "It's an enormous owl, Césare!" (Smisurato means "huge and out of proportion")
3. "The boss here."
4. helicopter

quickly," he added, putting the little radio back in his coat pocket.

The four Interpol cat teams glued their eyes to the approaching big owl. Frieda-K circled the transmitter tower at the Vatican radio station, flared her wings, lowered her tail feathers and landed. Gracefully. And right in front of the sleeping Fred-X. She was so stealthy he didn't even wake up. Frieda-K apparently decided to let him sleep. She snuggled up next to him and dozed over, herself.

✳ ✳ ✳

Over the North Atlantic—Above Iceland

The cabin of the sleek *The Flying Pig Machine* was almost silent as they finished their climb out of Gander. Dusty had set a course that would take the little Sabreliner and its five adventurers north over Iceland before turning back to the southeast on a straight line to Rome and the big international airport, *Fiumicino*.

Luigi and Luisa, full of energy, were playing their favorite in-flight game. They called it "jumpseat." Perching on the top of a seat back, each would leap to the back of the next set of seats, hopping their way around the plane's cabin. With each jump, they would call out, "Ribbit, ribbit" as if they were frogs. The game, silly though it might be, kept the two little bundles of energy busy. For about fifteen minutes. Until they got bored.

Luisa's last leap for this round of jumpseat found her landing squarely in Buzzer's lap. She looked up at her startled big brother and asked, "Buzzy, tell us a story. Tell us about when you and Cincinnati first caught up with Fred-X. And then tricked him. Pleeeez!"

Luigi hopped down beside her on Buzzer's other knee and joined the pleading. "Yes, Buzzy, tell us *tutta la storia, per favore!*[5]. We need to know everything about that evil owl if we're going to be able to help you catch him. Right? We'll be your *investigatori più abile.*"[6]

Buzzer knew he had told this story to the kittens before, but he also knew how much the little ones loved to listen to stories. Any stories. So he agreed to tell it to them once again. After all, they had little else to do for the next four or five hours, anyway.

"*Allora, mici investigatori miei piccoli,*[7] here's how we met up with Fred-X," Buzzer began.

---

5. the whole history, please
6. most clever detectives
7. Well, then my little kitten detectives

"Once upon a time—three years ago—I had just retired as director of operations of the CIA. Dusty Louise, Dr. Buford Lewis and his very smart brother Bogart-BOGART and I had just moved into our new ranch house in the Texas hill country.

"One evening right after dinner I decided to go out to the barn to work on my hobby—building bird houses. Remember? So I was busy putting together a Martin house when all of a sudden a huge shadow came between my workbench and the light bulb overhead. A rush of wind blew some hay straw 'round and 'round like a dust devil. Before I could grab my hammer to protect myself, two pair of giant talons grabbed me and whisked me away into the night sky."

Luisa's eyes grew as big as walnuts. Luigi realized she was holding her breath. "Breathe, Luisa!" he interrupted. "Or you're going to pass out and miss the story." Luigi was more worried that his tiny twin sister might miss some of the excitement than that she might actually go unconscious from lack of oxygen.

Buzzer smiled at Luigi's concern and went on with the tale. "It was Fred-X, all right, and he had me tight in his grip. We flew higher and higher. Faster and faster. I could tell from the stars that we were heading northeast. I had read about this big owl who would steal cats and fly them to Memphis. It came in my secure CIA e-mail. So that's where I figured we were heading, for sure."

"What did you do, Buzzy? Did Fred-X take you all the way to Memphis? Is that a long way?" Luigi's eyes were growing bigger and bigger. But he was careful to keep breathing.

"Well, guys, I decided to play 'possum' to give me time to think up a plan. So I went limp. And while I was thinking, that stupid owl almost ran into a Delta 757 landing at Dallas/Fort Worth International Airport. I had to yell 'Watch out!' or we would have been sucked into a big jet engine and turned into sausage.

"Then, right over Hope, Arkansas, I started my plan. I tricked Fred-X into dropping me into the top of a big pine tree. Once he figured out I was loose from his grip, he crash landed like a pelican. Just couldn't find me again in the dark."

"Then how did Cincinnati meet him, Buzzy? Did he come to Arkansas?" Luisa, now breathing again, wanted to know.

"No, Luisa. I pretended to be a hobo and caught a freight train that took me all the way to Ohio. And that big bird followed me. Day and night. He seemed like he was either really stupid or he was determined to catch me and take me back to Memphis. His daytime job was delivering packages for an overnight express company. So I guessed somebody had told him I was a package that had to get to Memphis. Maybe.

"Well, Fred-X caught up with me in our dancing pig friend's hometown of Cincinnati. So I asked my old buddy to help me trick this bird once and for all." Buzzer winked at his sidekick, who had left his pilot's seat and come back to the little plane's galley for a snack.

"What did you guys do?" Luigi wanted to hear the plot.

"We decided to play Fred-X's game and trap him that way, Luigi. Cincinnati actually flew me to Memphis. There he packed me into an overnight parcel box and addressed it to our new little ranch house in the hill country. He dropped a hint here and a bribe there. And he managed to arrange for Fred-X to be the one to deliver the package. Just as we got near the new ranch house, I pulled a cord and the package burst open.

Fireworks went off. Whistles and sirens blared. A silk parachute took me safely to the ground. But Fred-X was terrified. He crash-landed and begged for mercy. So I made him promise to leave the country and never steal a cat. Ever again.

"He did, too. Leave the country, that is. Went south to Mexico and Central America and must have behaved himself for a long time. But I guess old habits eventually come back. That's when Vicente Fox, president of Mexico, called us to save the cats of his country.

"And you know the rest."

"Wow, Buzzer. You and Cincinnati must be really tired of Fred-X by now," Luigi said thoughtfully. "This time we'll get him for sure. Maybe we'll give him cement shoes and drop him in *il fiume Tevere*[8]. That's the big river that runs through Rome, isn't it Buzzy?" Luigi smiled at the solution he'd seen in an old Jimmy Cagney movie on TNT.

"You've got to stop watching those old black-and-white gangster movies, Luigi." It was Cincinnati, heading back to the pilot's chair, smiling at the imagination of the little kitten who obviously watched too much television.

"We don't use cement shoes, Luigi. But we'll catch that owl. You can bet on it," Cincinnati assured him.

"Meantime I suggest you two little *mici*[9] get some sleep. Take a nap, Luigi and Luisa." Cincinnati almost commanded them before he noticed that Luisa was already snoozing away and Luigi was yawning, headed fast for dreamland.

✳   ✳   ✳

---

8. the Tiber River
9. kittens

Fiumicino International Airport—Rome

As the little jet landed, Cincinnati the dancing pig once again turned the controls over to Dusty Louise to taxi to the Jet-Sweep terminal. That's where Césare had said the group from Interpol would meet to "plot and plan." Or so Luigi had reported.

Sure enough, Césare was there. Waiting for them to get off the plane. He shoved his yellow straw fedora back off his forehead. Césare looked worried as the Sabreliner's front door opened and the stairs came down.

"C'mon out, team." Cincinnati called to Buzzer, Dusty, and the little twins. "Césare's here to meet us. But he doesn't look happy."

What do you suppose Césare's worried about? Or is he just tired from so many hours of owl watching? Will Cincinnati and Dusty be too tired to "plot and plan?" What about Buzzer and the *mici gemelli?*[10] Did they take long enough naps to be able to think clearly?

---

10. kitten twins

Impariamo un po' d'Italiano.

(We're Going to Learn a Little Italian.)

By Luisa Manicotti Giaccomazza

If you're going to travel around in Italy like we're about to do, you'll need to know some of the words about going from one place to another.

In English	In Italian	Say It Like This
Airplane	*aeroplano*	ah-air-oh-PLAHN-oh
Helicopter	*elicottero*	ehl-ee-COAT-tair-oh
Train	*treno*	TREN-oh
Car	*macchina*	MOCK-ee-nah
Bus	*autobus*	ah-OO-toh-boose
Boat	*barca*	BAHR-cah
Ship	*nave*	NAH-veh
Truck	*camion*	cah-mee-OHN
Pickup	*camioncino*	cah-mee-ohn-CHEE-noh
Bicycle	*bicicletta*	bee-chee-CLAY-tah

And you'll need to know where these various kinds of transportation may be found.

Road	*strada*	STRAH-dah
Freeway/Highway	*autostrada*	aw-toh-STRAH-dah
Street	*via*	VEE-ah
River	*fiume*	fee-OO-meh
Stream	*corrente*	cohr-REN-teh
Sea	*mare*	MAHR-eh
Path	*sentiero*	sen-tee-AIR-oh
Sidewalk	*marciapiede*	mahr-chah-pee-AID-eh
Airport	*aeroporto*	ah-air-oh-POHR-toh

Part Two

Owls on the Loose in Italy

"I wish *il Papa** would tend to his own business
and leave the owl-catching to
the real owl-catchers."

—Cincinnati
the dancing pig

---

* the pope

* Chapter 4 *
Lo Ha Fatto Il Papa[1]

Jet-Sweep "Plot and Plan" Room—Fiumicino in Rome

Luigi spoke first. Directly to his cousin, Césare Pepperoni Giaccomazza. Césare had taken off his yellow straw hat and set it on the conference room table. A sure sign something was up. Something that wouldn't be good. And he looked worried.

"Perché sei tanto preoccupato, cugino?"[2] Luigi asked the obvious.

"Io non sono preoccupato, Luigi. Stanco, forse, ma non preoccupato, cugino."[3]

Dusty was upset. "Tell us what they're saying, Luisa!" she demanded. "Right now. I want to know. Do you hear me?" Dusty, who had thought herself queen cat interpreter in Mexico, just couldn't bear the thought that Luigi and Luisa knew what was being said. And she didn't.

"Chill, Dusty," Luisa said, secretly laughing to herself at

---

1. The Pope Did It
2. "Why are you so worried, cousin?"
3. "I'm not worried, Luigi. Tired, maybe, but not worried, cousin."

Dusty's frantic demands. "Luigi asked Césare why he was so worried. And Césare said he's not worried. Maybe a little tired, but not worried. There. Is that what you wanted to know?" Luisa just loved the thought of knowing something—anything—that Dusty didn't know.

Buzzer stepped into the conversation. It was time to get a briefing. And never mind the little battle of wits between Luisa and Dusty.

"Tell us what's happened today, Césare. Please," Buzzer asked.

Césare looked down at the tabletop. He put his two front paws together like a steeple in front of him. Then he looked up directly at Buzzer and shocked everyone in the room. Everyone except *Tenente* Poni. She already knew what was coming.

"Fred-X and Frieda-K have slipped through our paws. They

got away. For a while." Césare said. He looked around the room as the shock registered on every face.

"How?" Cincinnati had but one one-word question.

"*Lo ha fatto il Papa. Mi dispiace.*"[4]

Luisa translated immediately. She knew after hearing

---

4. "The pope did it. I'm sorry."

this news it was no time to play games. He said, "'The Pope did it.' Césare's sorry."

"How? And why?" Cincinnati now had two one-word questions.

"Perhaps *Tenente* Poni should tell you. Her English is a little better than mine. But, please. Don't worry. *Non ti preoccupare, per favore.*[5] Everything is under control." Césare looked to Poni and nodded as if to say, "Go ahead."

"Here's how it happened," Poni began. "But *primo*[6]—ah, first—please understand we know where the *due gufi*[7] are. They are, how would you say, Luisa?"

"Under surveillance?" Luisa offered.

"*Sí, sí. Certo*[8]. They are 'under surveillance.' We know where they are, and we have two teams—eight agents—following them. Right now. So, don't worry."

"How did they get away in the first place?" Cincinnati was sticking stubbornly to his first two questions.

"It happened like this," Poni started again to try to explain. "If you will all let me finish, *per favore*,[9] then I will try to answer all these questions.

"Césare had four teams watching from rooftops all around the *piazza* in the front of the Vatican radio station. That's where Fred-X had landed and gone to sleep. A few hours later, Frieda-K joined him there. They both slept. We were watching the whole time. Every minute."

Buzzer interrupted. "Please, Poni. You don't worry. We

---

5. Don't worry, please.
6. first
7. two owls
8. Yes, yes. Of course.
9. please

know how slippery Fred-X can be. And nobody's blaming you. Or Césare. Or Interpol. We just want to know what happened. What you know right now. And then we'll all decide where we go from here, OK?"

"*Grazie, signor gatto nero-e-bianco.*"[10] Poni continued. "As I was saying, we watched these two *gufi* all night long. In the middle of the morning—and we don't know why—the Pope went for a little walk over by the radio station. We saw him coming, but there was nothing we could do. As you know, we were really trespassing in the Vatican. Maybe we should have told the Swiss Guard we would be there. They are the official *polizia*[11] of Vatican City, you know. But maybe they would have asked us to leave. Or not to come in the first place. Who knows?"

"Besides," Césare jumped in, "if they were really doing their jobs, they would have found us, anyway. I mean, eight cats, a helicopter, heat-sensors, binoculars. On four rooftops. We were all over the place."

"Whatever, Césare." Poni looked at her boss as if to say, "You want me to explain this? Or do you want to? And why do I always have to be the one to deliver bad news, anyway?"

"Go ahead, Poni. *Mi scusi, per favore.*"[12]

"*Di niente, Césare.*[13] I will continue. As the Pope strolled past the front of the radio station with two assistants, suddenly Frieda-K jumped up and began pleading with him. Begging.

We couldn't hear what she was saying. But very quickly

---

10. "Thank you, Mr. black-and-white cat."
11. police
12. Excuse me, please.
13. "It's nothing, Césare.

the assistants whisked Fred-X and Frieda-K into the front door of the radio station. A few minutes later, a—*elicottero*, Luisa¿"

"Helicopter."

"Yes. A helicopter. It landed on the roof of the radio station. Fred-X and Frieda-K were shoved aboard. And it took off immediately. We, of course, followed it in our own helicopter."

"Where did they go¿" Dusty was getting impatient. As only Dusty could do.

"To the *grande stazione dei treni*."[14]

"The large train station." Luisa was into this job of translating. Big time. Luigi looked at her proudly.

"Right," Poni continued. "The train station. Now they were on Italian soil—out of the Vatican—but we still hadn't received the fugitive warrant from Mexico for Fred-X. And Frieda-K had done nothing illegal. So we were forced to *osservare*[15]. Luisa¿"

"To watch them," Luisa responded immediately.

"*Sí.* To watch them. I believe you would say 'put them under surveillance,' no¿"

"Yes, *tenente*. You put them under surveillance." Luisa looked at Dusty. She didn't really stick out her tongue and give Dusty a razzberry, but the look she gave her older sister had the same effect. Dusty just looked away and pretended not to notice.

"Let's cut to the chase, please, lieutenant." Buzzer was getting a little impatient to find out where the two owls were right now. "Do you have the fugitive warrant from Mexico yet¿ And where are those two big birds¿"

---

14. the big railroad station
15. to watch, to observe

"Yes, the warrant came a few hours ago. And the two *grandi uccelli*[16] are on a train. A local train that makes many stops. They bought tickets for Bolzano. Near the Austrian border."

Cincinnati looked at Poni. Then at Césare. "I assume you have agents on the train. And at the many stations along the way?" he asked.

"*Certo signor maialino danzatore.*[17] We are Interpol. We are professional. And we are on the job, you may be sure." Poni was not amused at the tone of Cincinnati's question.

"No offense, lieutenant," Cincinnati reacted. "I know Interpol is first rate. I just want to know where we are in this case. And it seems like it's taking a long time to find out."

"Then I shall conclude my remarks—*presto.*[18] Poni was still bristling.

"Yes, Cincinnati, we have four agents on the train. Four more are in a helicopter. They're flying from *stazione a stazione*[19] so they can meet the train to be sure the owls don't get off along the way. Or, if they do, to be able to arrest Fred-X and detain Frieda-K as a, how would you call it, a 'material witness,' I think.

"Before someone else asks, please, I can tell you the train is approaching Firenze right now. It's scheduled to be there *alle ventidue. In dieci minuti.*[20]

Luigi had been too quiet far too long. He piped up, "The

---

16. big birds
17. "Certainly, Mr. dancing pig."
18. quickly
19. station to station
20. at twenty-two hundred. In ten minutes

train is due in Florence in ten minutes at ten o'clock P.M.," he said. "But it'll probably be late. Trains always are."

"*Non in Italia, mio piccolo cugino. Puntuale. Esattamente. Il Duce Mussolini lo dice.*"[21] Césare offered a response . . . and a lesson in Italian train schedules for Luigi.

"He says the trains are not often late in Italy. They're on time. Exactly. Mussolini said so." Luisa smiled at Luigi as if to say, "Be careful, little brother, what you say in a foreign country."

"If their tickets are for Bolzano, then when will the train get there?" Buzzer was starting the "plot and plan" part of the meeting.

"*Alle undice di mattina,*"[22] Poni responded.

"Eleven o'clock tomorrow morning," Luisa translated. "In about thirteen more hours."

"Césare, how long is the runway at the Bolzano airport?" Cincinnati was thinking ahead.

"How long do you need to stop your beautiful plane, Cincinnati?" Césare responded.

"To be safe, at least fifteen hundred meters," Cincinnati answered.

"*Bene. Non c'e problema.* The main runway at Bolzano is at least fifteen hundred meters long," Césare said. "*Io penso,*"[23] he added.

"I know where you're going with that question," Buzzer said as he looked at Cincinnati. "We have some time to deal with 'plotting and planning.' Why don't we all get a little

---

21. "Not in Italy, little cousin. On time. Exactly. Mussolini says so."
22. "At eleven o'clock in the morning."
23. "Good. No problem." . . . "I think."

something to eat? Then we can spend an hour or so planning a proper welcome for Fred-X and Frieda-K when they get to Bolzano. Anybody ready for a little break?"

"Let's go to our offices in the city," Césare offered. "I'll call ahead to order up a Roman dinner and get somebody to check the runway length in Bolzano for sure."

"We also have two agents checking to try to find out what kind of story those owls fed the Pope to get him to give them safe passage," Poni said. "I want to hear that *storia buffa*,[24] for sure."

What do you think Frieda-K told il Papa to get him to send them on their way in a special helicopter? Why are they going to Bolzano? Is there a chance the two owls will escape from the train between stations? What will Césare offer his guests for dinner?

---

24. funny business

Impariamo un po' d'Italiano.

(We're Going to Learn a Little Italian.)

By Luisa Manicotti Giaccomazza

Many people throughout the world have the same names, but they are said and spelled differently in different countries. My name—Luisa—is Italian. In English, I would be called Louise. And Luigi would be Louis. Césare would be Caesar. Here are a few more for you.

In English	In Italian	Say It Like This
Ann	Anna	AHN-nah
Barbara	Barbara	BAHR-bah-rah
Charles	Carlo	CAR-loh
Christopher	Cristoforo	crees-TOH-foh-roh
David	Davide	dah-VEE-deh
Deborah	Debora	DAY-bore-ah
Dominick	Domenico	doh-MEHN-ee-coh
Edward	Eduardo	ay-DWAHR-doh
Elaine	Elena	ay-LAY-nah
Elizabeth	Elisabetta	ay-liss-ah-BET-tah
Frank	Franco	FRAHN-coh
Frances	Francesca	frahn-CHESS-cah
George	Giorgio	JOHR-joe
Hope	Speranza	spare-AHN-sah
Irene	Irene	ee-RAY-neh
James	Giacomo	JAH-coh-moh
Joseph	Guisseppe	jew-SEP-peh
Joe	Beppe	BEP-peh
John	Giovanni	joe-VAHN-nee

Louis	Luigi	loo-EE-gee
Louise	Luisa	loo-EE-sah
Linda	Linda	LEEN-dah
Lina	Lina	LEE-nah
Margaret	Margarita	mahr-gar-EE-tah
Mark	Marco	MAHR-coh
Martha	Marta	MAHR-tah
Mary	María	mah-REE-ah
Matthew	Matteo	maht-TAY-oh
Molly	Amalia	ah-MAH-lya
Peter	Pietro	pee-AY-troh
Richard	Riccardo	reek-CAHR-doh
Rose	Rosa	ROH-sah
Sarah	Sara	SAH-rah
Sophia	Sofia	soh-FEE-ah
Sylvia	Silvia	SEEL-vee-ah
Thomas	Tommáso	toh-MAHS-oh
Tommy	Tommasino	tohm-mah-SEE-noh
Victor	Vittorio	vee-TOHR-ee-oh
William	Guglielmo	gool-YELL-moh

* Chapter 5 *
When in Rome

"Benvenuti.[1] Welcome to our offices, *amici."*[2]

Césare led the small procession down a dimly lit hallway on the fourth floor of a very old building near the center of Rome—about a city block from the *Piazza Navona* and not too far from the famous Spanish Steps.

"Come on into our conference room. Our assistants are preparing a Roman dinner for your refreshment and enjoyment." Césare smiled as he showed his cousins and friends from *Stati Uniti* into a big conference room with a long table down the middle. The table had been set with fine china and crystal. A brilliant white tablecloth covered the entire surface. And candles were lit in three candle holders along the center.

"Luisa, this is going to be a feast. *Ho fame,"*[3] Luigi rubbed his stomach and licked his lips.

"*Anche io,*[4] Luigi. But try to remember your manners. Let's

---

1. Welcome
2. friends

3. I'm hungry.
4. Me, too.

just be sure Cincinnati is the only pig at the table. Know what I mean?" Luisa smiled at her little brother.

As the group took their places around the table, Buzzer remained standing. He raised his water glass as if to offer a toast. And he spoke directly to Césare and Tenente Poni. "We thank you for your hard work over the past twenty-four hours. And we thank you for this hospitality. Especially a fine meal served so late at night. That must have been a lot of extra trouble."

Buzzer lowered his glass and the group applauded softly.

"*Non c'é problema,*[5] Buzzer," Poni responded. "Actually it is only a little later than usual for dinner in Roma. Here we eat very late in the evening."

"Why is that, Poni?" Luigi was curious. As usual.

Poni looked at the twins and smiled. "Most days, when we're not watching evil owls, our schedules are very different from yours in *Stati Uniti*," she said. "We go to work about eight o'clock in the morning. But at noon we take three or four hours off—for a light meal, some rest and to spend time with our families. Even the stores close *a mezzogiorno.*[6] Then we go back to work at about fifteen-thirty or sixteen hundred hours. You would say 'three-thirty or four o'clock,' I believe. And we work until maybe twenty hundred hours. That's eight in the evening. So our *pranzo,*[7] our dinner, usually does not begin until the hour of nine-thirty or ten o'clock.

---

5. "No problem, Buzzer."   7. dinner
6. at noon

"So it is not so late for us. But you must be very hungry," she smiled.

Luigi noticed that Dusty Louise was staring at Poni. Staring to the point of almost seeming to be in a trance. He turned to Luisa and whispered, "Look at Dusty. She's staring daggers right through the *tenente*. I wonder what that's all about?"

"So you just now noticed that, Luigi? She's been staring since we got off the plane almost two hours ago. I know what's going on here." She smiled at Luigi. She would make him ask her for more. Two could play Luigi's little game of wits.

"Luisa, don't act like me. Tell me! What's Dusty's problem?"

"Well, Luigi, now that you ask, I'll tell you what I think. I think there's going to be big trouble between Dusty and the *tenente* unless Buzzer steps in and puts his foot down. Hard. Right on Dusty's cute little neck."

"You think she's jealous?" Luigi asked.

"Of course she is, Luigi. Look at it this way. Dusty's used to being the most beautiful cat in the room. Wherever she is. And she is pretty. No doubt about that. But this *Tenente* Poni is gorgeous, no? Dusty's suddenly not the queen bee. And it's making her squirm," Luisa concluded.

"Will you keep an eye on the two of them, Luisa? I'm going to be too busy being *l' investigatore piú abile*.[8] But I don't want to miss any of the fireworks."

Luisa just looked at Luigi, shook her head and rolled her eyes. "Why is it that guys can only do one thing at a time?" she wondered to herself.

But Luigi was already on to the next subject. "What kind

---

8. most clever detective

of food do you eat here in Rome?" he asked Césare. "Is it all going to be strange stuff?"

Césare laughed. "No, *cugino*. It will not be strange, I think. At *pranzo*[9] we'll serve several plates. The first will be either a soup or a pasta. We call that *il primo piatto*[10]. Then we will serve *il secondo piatto*[11] of meat or fish and some vegetables. We'll finish up with an *insalata*[12] and some *frutta*[13]. Sometimes we even begin with something sweet. What I believe you would call 'dessert' *in inglese, no?*[14]" And of course, there is always wine—*vino*."

"Dessert first? Wow!" Luigi was paying attention now. "Well, Luisa, you know what they say: 'When in Rome, eat dessert first.'"

Everyone laughed at Luigi's remark except Dusty. She was pouting. Pretending she didn't understand any of the Italian being spoken. "Really, she can understand everything," Luisa whispered to Luigi. "She's just looking at Poni and feeling . . . well, feeling like a normal good-looking cat instead of the belle of the ball. Ha!"

Luisa was enjoying watching Dusty squirm. Dusty often made fun of the little twins. And seldom went out of her way to be nice to them. Luigi and Luisa just pretended she was the wicked stepsister. The one from *Cinderella*. And blew off her bad behavior. "It's the best way to deal with a spoiled brat, Luigi," she had assured her brother.

---

9. dinner
10. the first plate
11. the second plate

12. salad
13. fruit
14. in English, no?

Two men in white dinner jackets walked into the room. One took a note directly to Poni. The other pushed a cart with dishes that smelled wonderful. As the *tenente* read the note, both *camerieri*[15] began to place small bowls of soup and salad plates with something on them that looked like large rings covered with pepper and oil.

Césare spoke up. "The soup is *zuppa di tortellini con formaggio in brodo*.[16] Small shell pasta stuffed with fine cheese and cooked in broth. And those rings on the small plates are what we call *calamari in olio d'oliva*[17]. Both are typical Italian dishes. Try them. I think you'll like them."

Luigi did. Like them, that is. He was eating away as Lieutenant Poni tapped her crystal wine glass with a spoon to get everyone's attention.

"Now we have at least part of the answer to the strange behavior of *il Papa*," she announced. "Our friends at the Swiss Guard in the Vatican have informed us that Frieda-K told the Pope a most remarkable tale. She claimed to be a nun of the order of Saint Swithen. And said that Fred-X was a monsignor—a Jesuit. Seems she claimed they were a nun and priest who had been turned into giant birds by a heretic televangelist. But they had escaped and needed to get back to the abbey in Bolzano to be returned to their former selves. She asked the Pope to pray for them. And to help them get secretly to the railroad station."

"And he bought that cockamamie story?" Luigi was having a hard time believing this tale.

---

15. waiters
16. soup of cheese-filled tortellini pasta in broth
17. squid marinated in olive oil

"Well, Luigi, that's what the Swiss Guard captain told my assistant. They said they were very sorry. Seems the Pope was not so sure about their wild tale, but one of the cardinals with him convinced him of its truth. Our friend said this particular cardinal is very suspicious of clergy who beg for money on television."

"As well he might be." Luigi blurted out. "But better keep an eye on that cardinal, though. He may be a bird of the same feather as Fred-X."

"You are becoming *un' investigatore più abile*,[18] Luigi. That's exactly what the captain of the Swiss Guard told us in secret. He thinks this cardinal's elevator really might not go all the way to the top floor. If you know what I mean. They're watching him. For their own reasons. And to be sure he doesn't get in our way when we go after Fred-X and Frieda-K tomorrow," Poni said.

Luigi smiled. He wanted, more than anything, to help capture Fred-X again. Even more important, he wanted to finish the great meal he'd just started. Being *un' investigatore più abile* could wait for a few minutes. Until he'd eaten all his delicious late Roman dinner.

With the dishes cleared away, Césare was peeling oranges and passing slices down and around the table.

"These oranges are red," Luisa whispered to Luigi. "But they're really tasty, I must say. What do you think makes them so red?"

"It's the blood of a million Roman legions spilled on the soil of the orchard where they grow." Luigi always had an answer. Sometimes his answers even amused Luisa.

---

18. clever detective

* When in Rome *

This was not one of those times.

Tenente Poni stood and spoke directly to Buzzer and Cincinnati the dancing pig. But she was speaking loudly enough for all to hear. "We have arranged for rooms for all of you at the Pension Texas. It's down the street. It's a small what you might call 'bed and breakfast'—an out-of-the-way place where you can get some rest without alerting anyone who may be looking out for the interests of Fred-X. You'll be ... what is the word, Luisa?"

"Incognito?" Luisa offered.

"Si, si. Incognito.[19] That's the same word as in Italian." Poni looked puzzled for a minute and then added, *"Come 'pizza.'"*[20]

Buzzer looked at Dusty and the twins and answered the question one of them, likely Luigi, was about to ask. "Césare and *Tenente* Poni will pick us up early in the morning. We'll fly directly to Bolzano. That is, if the two big birds are still on the train. And on the way, we'll finish 'plotting and planning.' How's that?

"Meantime," he continued, "we need to get a little rest. Especially Cincinnati and Dusty. We thank you for the wonderful dinner, Césare and Poni."

Did you ever eat dinner at midnight? Why do you think the Pope believed Frieda-K's strange story? Do you think maybe the cardinal is in cahoots with Fred-X? And what about the two big birds? Will they stay on the train all night? And why are they *really* going to Bolzano? Or are they?

---

19. Incognito
20. "Like 'pizza.'"

Impariamo un po' d'italiano

(We're Going to Learn a Little Italian.)

By Luisa Manicotti Giaccomazza

You've already seen that an owl's called a *gufo* in Italian. And cats are *gatti*. Kittens are *mici*. What are the Italian names for some other animals?

In English	In Italian	Say It Like This
Bear	*orso*	OHR-soh
Bird	*uccello*	oo-CHELL-oh
Cat	*gatto*	GAHT-toh
Cats	*gatti*	GAHT-tee
Cow	*mucca*	MOO-cah
Deer	*cervo*	CHAIR-voh
Dog	*cane*	CAH-neh
Donkey	*asino*	ah-SEE-noh
Eagle	*aquila*	ah-KWEE-lah
Fox	*volpe*	VOHL-peh
Goat	*capra*	CAH-prah
Horse	*cavallo*	cah-VAHL-loh
Kitten	*micio*	MEE-choh
Kittens	*mici*	MEE-chee
Lion	*leone*	lay-OHN-eh
Monkey	*scimmia*	SHIM-myah
Owl	*gufo*	GOO-foh
Owls	*gufi*	GOO-fee
Parrot	*pappagallo*	pah-pah-GAHL-loh
Pig	*maiale*	my-YAHL-eh
Rabbit	*coniglio*	coh-NEE-lyo

* When in Rome *

Sheep	*pecora*	PECK-oh-rah
Skunk	*puzzola*	pootz-ZOH-lah
Snake	*serpente*	sair-PEN-teh
Tiger	*tigre*	TEE-greh
Turtle	*tartaruga*	tar-tah-ROO-gah
Wolf	*lupo*	LOO-poh

* Chapter 6 *
North by Northwest

True to their word, Césare and *Tenente* Poni picked up *i quattro gatti*[1] and Cincinnati very early the next morning. They drove a big black bulletproof Fiat SUV. Luigi recognized the driver as one of the *camerieri*[2] from dinner at the Interpol office last night.

"*Buona mattinata, amici,*"[3] Césare greeted the visitors from America. "There won't be much traffic this early in the morning. We'll be at the Jet-Sweep terminal in about a half hour."

"What's up with Fred-X and Frieda-K?" Buzzer asked. He wanted to avoid small talk and get to the job at hand.

"At last report, they were still on the train as it was approaching Verona, Buzzer. They've been sleeping all night, our agent tells us. They've made no attempt to escape enroute."

"Good," Buzzer responded. "Cincinnati, how far is Bolzano? How long to get there?"

---

1. the four cats
2. waiters
3. "Good morning, friends."

"Figure about seven hundred kilometers," Cincinnati said. "A little under two hours flying time. Once we're in the air, I'll set the autopilot and turn the controls over to Dusty Louise. That way we can all be in on the 'plotting and planning' session." He looked at his watch. "If we get off the ground by about seven A.M. we should be on the tarmac in Bolzano before nine. Two hours ahead of the train and its special bird passengers."

Buzzer, Cincinnati, and Dusty Louise all looked a bit tired. Their eyes were bloodshot and had bags under them. Luigi and Luisa, though, were rested. And ready to go.

"What is this Bolzano place?" Luigi, ever curious, asked nobody in particular.

"It's a city in the north of Italy, Luigi," Poni answered. "In the Trentino region. Bolzano is near the south end of the Brenner Pass. We call it *Passo del Brennero*. *Brennero* is the pass in the *Dolomites*—the Italian Alps—where Hannibal passed through with his elephants hundreds of years ago. Do you know that story, Luigi?"

"Will there be elephants there?" Luisa suddenly became interested in the conversation.

"No, Luisa. I don't think so," Poni answered. "I think they've all gone back to Africa. But it is a beautiful city. There are mountainside vineyards and fruit orchards all around the town. And there is an abbey there. We had our agents check with the abbot early this morning to see if there might be a nun or a monsignor missing. And, of course, nobody was missing. The abbot was most interested in why we inquired. We had to promise to tell him later."

"Is there a Costello at this abbey?" Luigi asked.

"A Costello? *Io non capisco.*[4] What is a Costello, Luisa?" Luigi had confused the *tenente.*

Luisa laughed. "Luigi watches too many old movies on television, *tenente,*" she said. "He really likes gangster stories and the old Abbott and Costello comedies. Abbott and Costello are two funny guys who made movies a million years ago. Don't be confused, Poni." She turned to Luigi. "An abbot is the head of the abbey. It's where priests live. And make wine, I'll bet."

"I knew that." Luigi was quick to respond. "I was just checking to see if the *tenente* could pass for a real American, even if she was a spy." He smiled. Fooling everyone but Luisa, who just knew he made up that story on the spot.

Their driver raced through the light downtown traffic and hit the *autostrada*[5] to the airport at full speed.

"These Romans drive like maniacs," Luisa thought to herself.

Luigi, reading her mind, whispered, "I'll bet this guy was a race car driver, Luisa. Before he became a waiter. And an Interpol agent. Did you see what he did back there? He passed a bus and taxi by driving up on the sidewalk. *Mamma mía!*"[6]

As they pulled up to the Jet-Sweep terminal, they saw a small tractor slowly pulling *The Flying Pig Machine* from its overnight parking space to the front door of the terminal.

"Looks like they're ready for us," Césare said. *"Andiamo."*[7]

"You take the controls, Dusty." Cincinnati the dancing pig slipped out of his seat belt and stood in the cockpit of *The Flying Pig Machine.* "Remember, we're on autopilot, Dusty. You just watch what's happening and let me know if we get any

---

4. I don't understand.
5. freeway, highway

6. Goodness gracious!
7. "Let's go."

red lights or anything starts to blink at you, OK?" He leaned over and whispered, "I'll let everyone think you're flying the plane all by yourself. Even though we both know you're not ready to do that yet. I know that something about that *tenente* is bugging you. Right?"

Dusty smiled and gave him a high five. "I'll be fine, Cincinnati. You go 'plot and plan.' I'll just watch what's happening up here and yell out if anything goes haywire." She thought to herself, "I'll bet that calico rag doll can't fly an airplane. Or speak Spanish. Some things are more important than just being beautiful. Besides, I'm not so bad looking, myself, am I? No!"

Cincinnati stopped by the galley and picked up a can of *aranciata*.[8] He popped it open, took a gulp and wandered on back into the cabin where Buzzer Louis, Césare, the *tenente*, and Luigi and Luisa were waiting to get on with 'plotting and planning.'

"How's the plan coming along?" Cincinnati sat down next to Luigi.

"We've been waiting for you, *signor maialino danzatore*,"[9] Césare said as looked up and pushed back the brim of his jaunty yellow fedora. "We have them outnumbered about eight to one. Besides the seven of us, we have the four agents on the train and the four following the train along in our helicopter. So there are fifteen of us, plus our pilot, to capture two owls," he said.

8. orange-flavored soft drink
9. mister dancing pig

"Yes, *cugino*, but remember those two owls can fly," Luigi said. "I can't fly. And I don't think any of you can fly. I might be wrong about that. But I'm not wrong very much of the time."

"Yes, Buzzer," Luisa said, looking at her big brother. "What do we do if they take off flying?"

"We'll have the Interpol helicopter," Césare said. "But our pilot is going to be too tired to go far. Remember, he's been flying all night."

"*Non c'é problema*,[10] Césare," Luigi beamed. "Cincinnati can fly the helicopter. Right, Cincinnati?"

"It's true. I can do that." He spoke up a little more loudly and turned toward the cockpit. "With Dusty doing all the flying this morning, I'll be rested and ready if we need to use the whirlybird. What kind is it, Césare?"

"It's big and green and runs on jet fuel." Césare looked a little perplexed. And he looked to *Tenente* Poni to add some details.

"It is an Aerospatiale twin engine, Cincinnati. It will hold up to thirteen passengers," Poni said. "Can you fly it?"

"Well, I'm not too keen on French machines, to tell the truth, Poni. But I have been checked out in most of the Aerospatiale 'copters. NATO flies some of them, you know. Can we contact your pilot and have him be sure it's fueled up as soon as he lands in Bolzano? Just in case?"

"Césare opened his small *cartella*,[11] took out a paper and unfolded it. "Here's a map of the area around the *stazione*[12] in

---

10. "No problem."
11. briefcase
12. railroad station

Bolzano," he said. "Here you can see it's right in the middle of the city. Big buildings all around. The only escape route is to the east, where there's the *Adige* River and the *autostrada*. There is a small *piazza* in front of the station, but it's used by cars, buses, and taxis. I'll have four agents on the east side of the terminal. The four on the train will fan out and surround the owls as they get off—one each on the north, south, east, and west. That leaves us to confront Fred-X and Frieda-K. But when? And where? It will be the middle of the day— *mezzogiorno*—noon. And there'll be a lot of people walking around. Especially near the railroad station. What do you think, Buzzer?"

Buzzer studied the map. "I've seen better setups for a capture," he said. "Cincinnati, don't you think Césare and the *tenente* should be the ones to face off against Fred-X? The rest of us need to stay out of sight until the very last second. Right?"

"Absolutely, Buzzer," Cincinnati shook his head "yes." He looked at Luigi and Luisa, who were starting to fidget. "Want to explain why, guys?" he asked.

"Obviously," Luisa began to explain, "Fred-X knows all of us. He's especially scared of Buzzer and Cincinnati. But even if he only sees Luigi or me, he'll know Buzzer's here. And Cincinnati. And he'll freak."

Luigi piped up, "A freaked-out owl in a crowded railroad station is not something we want to see. Not today. In fact," he added, standing up to try to look bigger, "we don't ever want to see a freaked-out owl. I've seen it. It's not a pretty sight. Trust me."

"Right, Luigi," Buzzer said to the little kitten's total delight. "I think we have our best chance if we can nab those two inside the station. Quickly. Cleanly. Before they can get to daylight where they might try to fly away. So here's what I think we should do."

Buzzer took out a pencil and began to sketch lightly on the map. "See? Everyone will have a position to hold. All the exits will be blocked. We should have them bottled up tight. Any questions? Anybody worried about anything? OK, then, we have almost an hour before we touch down at Bolzano. I want everybody to close their eyes and each of us try to imagine what we'll do when the train stops at the station. Think exactly what you'll do."

"Why are we doing this?" Luigi wanted to know.

"Practice, Luigi. We want to be ready when we meet that train. And all the Interpol agents won't be with us until it arrives. So we have to imagine what we're going to do. See it in our mind's eye. Understand?"

"*Si, si, mio generale.*"[13] Luigi snapped to attention and saluted. And promptly fell backward off the seat onto the floor. He looked up as everyone started to laugh. "Practice, practice, practice," he said, grinning at himself.

Do you think Dusty Louise should be piloting *The Flying Pig Machine* while she's so upset about Poni? Even though it's on autopilot? Will our team of owl-catchers need to use the French helicopter? Will Cincinnati be able to fly it if they do? And what about Buzzer Louis's plan? Do you think it will work? In a crowded railroad station in the middle of the day?

---

13. "Yes, yes, my general."

Impariamo un po' d'Italiano.

(We're Going to Learn a Little Italian.)

By Luisa Manicotti Giaccomazza

When you travel where Italian is spoken, you'll want to eat when you're hungry. Here are some common foods and how to say them in Italian.

In English	In Italian	Say It Like This
Bread	pane	PAH-neh
Butter	burro	BOO-roh
Jelly	marmellata	mahr-mehl-LAH-tah
Cheese	formaggio	for-MAH-joe
Milk	latte	LAH-teh
Bacon	pancetta	pahn-CHET-tah
Egg	uovo	WHOA-voh
Vegetables	verdure	vair-DURE-reh
Potato	patata	pah-TAH-tah
Tomato	pomodoro	poh-moh-DOHR-oh
Bean	fagiolo	fah-JOH-loh
Beans	fagioli	fah-JOH-lee
Corn	granturco	grahn-TOOR-coh
Salad	insalata	een-sah-LAH-tah
Sandwich	panino	pah-NEE-noh
Water	acqua	OCK-wah
Mineral water	acqua minerale	Ock-wah meen-air-AH-leh
Soup	zuppa	ZOOP-pah
Beef	manzo	MAHN-zoh
Ham	prosciutto	pro-SHOOT-toh
Pork	maiale	my-AHL-eh

Chicken	*pollo*	POH-loh
Rabbit	*coniglio*	coh-NEE-lyo
Venison	*carne di cervo*	CAHR-neh dee CHAIR-voh
Fruit	*frutta*	FROOT-tah
Apple	*mela*	MEH-lah
Orange	*arancia*	ah-RAHN-chah
Orange soda	*aranciata*	ah-rahn-CHAH-tah
Banana	*banana*	bah-NAH-nah
Strawberry	*fragola*	FRAH-goh-lah
Pear	*pera*	PAIR-rah
Peanuts	*arachidi*	ahr-rah-KEY-dee
Cookie	*biscotto*	bees-COAT-toh
Cake	*torta*	TOHR-tah
Candy	*caramella*	cahr-ah-MEL-lah
Ice cream	*gelato*	gee-LAH-toh

* Chapter 7 *
An Incident Most Curious

In the Air Over Central Italy

Tired of closing their eyes and practicing, *i mici gemelli*[1] had begun yet another game of jump-seat. Luigi was trying to leap across two seats in one jump. Just to spice up what otherwise might be a game too tame. When he missed and crashed into a seat back, knocking off Césare's little yellow straw hat, he decided to stop the game and try something else. Before he got into trouble.

"Tell us another story, Buzzer. Pleeez!" he said.

"Yes, Buzzy. Tell us about you and Cincinnati at Cats-in-Action—the CIA. Tell all of us about one of your famous adventures." Luisa joined the pleading.

"I don't know, guys. I've told you about all the stories I know. About how we captured Carlos the Puma in Argentina. About heading off the Middle Eastern assassin in the Vatican.

---

1. the kitten twins

The one trying to plant plastic explosives in the little Mercedes popemobile. And about scaring the little mouse under the chair in Buckingham Palace, remember? When the queen made me a knight. Even about Cincinnati's heroics in Hong Kong when we brought the evil opium-smuggling panda Ar Chee to justice. I'm just about out of stories. At least short stories. We're going to be in Bolzano in a half hour, you know."

"I'll tell you one I'll bet you've never heard." It was Cincinnati, still sipping his *aranciata*[2] and just waiting for the autopilot to alert Dusty it was time to start their descent into Bolzano. "Buzzer probably hasn't told you about the 'Bulldog of Belgrade,' has he?"

"Noooo!" A chorus of two squeaky kitten voices filled the little plane's cabin with an ear-splitting shrillness that caused *Tenente* Poni to quickly cover her ears. "Tell us about the Bulldog, Cincinnati," Luisa said. She cocked her head and batted her eyelashes. And tried to look cute.

"OK. Sit down and stop leaping around the plane. I'll tell you about your brave big brother and how he solved a big, big problem for the sausage lovers of Europe.

Cincinnati thought for a minute. And then began the story. "Once upon a time about five years ago in September, Socks—the cat who's our boss at Cats-in-Action—sent Buzzer and me to Vienna to look into a very strange, but quite ugly, international scam. Seems the evil Bulldog of Belgrade was stealing sausages shipped from three different factories in Vienna . . ."

---

2. orange-flavored soft drink

"Vienna sausages?" Luigi shouted out. *"Mi piace molto la salsiccia viennese!*[3] Mmm."

"Yes, well, they are quite tasty, Luigi," Cincinnati continued. "But every time a truck left one of the plants in Vienna where the sausages were being made, it just disappeared. Thousands of boxes . . . millions of sausages never got to where they were being shipped. The trucks always turned up. Empty. And the truck drivers all claimed they had amnesia. Couldn't remember a thing. Except a bright light. No, a brilliant white light. And then, nothing. Nobody ever saw the Bulldog. Or any members of his gang."

"What happened to the sausages, Cincinnati? That Bulldog must really like to eat sausages. Lots of sausages." Luisa said.

"That's what Socks sent Buzzer and me to find out. At first we decided to hide in a truck and ride along to see what happened. But every time we went along, nothing happened. Not a thing. The truck just delivered the sausages. And that was that. It was almost like the sausage thieves somehow knew which trucks we were hiding in. Or so we thought.

"We needed a clever plan to get to the bottom of this giant Vienna sausage caper."

"What did you do, Cincinnati? What was the plan?" Luigi was sitting on the edge of his seat, eyes wide.

"Buzzer was really thinking, Luigi. He remembered that Oktoberfest was coming up in Munich. And where does the world eat more sausages than at Oktoberfest? In Munich? So we set up a sausage-eating contest and offered a big prize—a lifetime supply of wursts. You know, bratwurst, knockwurst.

---

3. "I really like Vienna sausages!"

Vienna sausages. All kinds. We thought anybody who was stealing sausages by the truckload would be sure to be a big sausage eater. And enter the contest."

"Did it work, Cincinnati?" Luisa asked.

"Perfectly, Luisa. The Bulldog was the first to enter. Contestant *numero uno*.[4] And you know what else? Two of the factory foremen from each of the three factories in Vienna also entered. We figured they must be the insiders tipping off the Bulldog and his gang.

"So we arranged for the Bulldog and the six foremen to sit at the same table at the contest. I took the other seat. Buzzer prepared special sausages for that table. Guaranteed to put the eater to sleep after three or four bites. And, shazam! We had the leader of the sausage-stealing gang—the Bulldog of Belgrade—and all six of his inside henchmen wrapped up in about five minutes. Neat. And clean."

"What about the lights, Cincinnati? You know, the brilliant white lights the drivers said they saw? What were they?" Luisa still had questions.

"The inside foremen would tip off the gang to the trucks' routes, Luisa. Then they would hide a time-delay flash flare in the cab of the truck. Those flares were rigged to not only light up in a big flash, but also to give off a gas that would cause the drivers to pass out for hours. It was a diabolical scheme. Of course, each time Buzzer and I would ride along, they couldn't hide the flares. They knew we would find them at once. Pretty clever, no?" Cincinnati asked.

"What happened to all the sausages they were stealing,

---

4. number one

Cincinnati? Surely they couldn't eat millions of sausages. Not even a big bulldog can eat that much." Luisa still had questions. She thought the dancing pig wasn't quite as good a storyteller as Buzzer. When Buzzer finished a story, she never had any more questions.

"They all ended up in Belgrade, Luisa. Sure, the Bulldog and his gang ate some of them. But they re-sold most of them into the black market in Asia. They called their exporting company 'Bulldog Sausages.' Sounds kind of yucky, right?"

"Asians do eat strange things, though," Luigi offered. And then changing the subject as only Luigi could do, he asked, "Who won?"

"Who won what, Luigi?" Cincinnati didn't understand the little kitten's question.

"The sausage-eating contest. Who won the sausage eating contest, of course?"

"Oh, sorry. You're not going to believe this, Luigi. We didn't. But the judges swore it was true. The contest was won by a skinny little poodle from Paris named Francois du Monde. He ate two hundred and fifty-seven sausages in fifteen minutes. And he also drank three quarts of beer."

"Wow! I'll bet he couldn't even walk, Cincinnati. He must've been more stuffed than any of the sausages he ate." Luigi was snickering.

"As a matter of fact, he had to be carried back to his hotel. But he was a proud, proud Frenchman. He'd out-eaten a Doberman, a German shorthaired pointer. Even a Siberian Husky and a big Russian weightlifter."

"Good job, Cincinnati," Buzzer said. "Those two just have to have their stories."

Dusty Louise peeked around the cockpit door. "Cincinnati, the GPS says we're right over a place called Trento. And I think that's where we're supposed to begin our approach into Bolzano. Isn't it?"

"Right-o, Dusty." Cincinnati got up and headed for the cockpit, leaving the rest of the "plotters and planners" in the passenger cabin of *The Flying Pig Machine*. Almost at once, everyone noticed he had spooled down the twin fanjets and put the little jet into a gradual slope downward.

Luigi peered out the window and down at the ground. "Look over there, Luisa." He pointed. "You can see the *autostrada* and the big *Adige* River and—look just ahead. That's smoke. And helicopters hovering. There're ambulances and fire trucks racing up the highway. Look, Luisa!"

Everyone gazed out one of the right-hand windows.

"*Curioso,*"[5] Césare offered. "I wonder what's going on? That big green helicopter down there looks like ours. Poni, get on that satellite phone and see if you can contact the Interpol whirlybird. See if they know what's happening. Something big time is going on down there."

"Everybody fasten your seat belts and bring your seatbacks upright. We're on our final approach. Thanks." Cincinnati spoke over the intercom.

"Bolzano tower, this is Sabreliner seven zero niner niner alpha. Forty kilometers to the south on direct requesting permission to land and a temporary parking space, please, sir." Dusty was getting a lot of experience talking to air traffic controllers.

---

5. "Curious," strange

"Sabreliner seven zero niner niner, this is Bolzano tower. You are cleared to land. Did you see any strange traffic as you passed north of Trento, Sabreliner? We see a lot of activity on radar. But we don't know what it is."

"Bolzano tower, there seemed to be a fire on the ground about ten kilometers north of Trento. A lot of helicopters in the area and emergency vehicles on the highway headed to the location. We're not sure what's happening."

"Thank you, Sabreliner. Taxi to the line east of the terminal. Secure your own wheel chocks, please. And welcome to Bolzano, miss."

What do you think the smoke might be? Was the helicopter Césare saw really the Interpol whirlybird? How do you think a poodle could eat so many sausages? So fast? Will the train be on time to Bolzano? Will Buzz's plan to arrest Fred-X in the train station really work?

Impariamo un po' d'Italiano.

(We're Going to Learn a Little Italian.)

By Luisa Manicotti Giaccomazza

How would you know what to wear if you were traveling in an Italian-speaking country? Here are the names of some articles of clothing you might want to bring with you or buy along the way.

In English	In Italian	Say It Like This
Shirt	camicia	cah-MEE-chah
Pants	pantaloni	pahn-tah-LOH-nee
Belt	cintura	cheen-TOOR-ah
Skirt	sottana	soat-TAH-nah
Blouse	blusa	BLOO-sah
Dress	vestito	ves-TEE-toh
Jacket	giacca	JOCK-cah
Coat	soprabito	soh-PRAH-bee-toh
Shoes	scarpe	SCAR-peh
Boots	stivali	stee-VAH-lee
Socks	calzine	cahl-ZEE-neh
Raincoat	impermeabile	eem-pear-mee-AH-bee-leh
Umbrella	ombrello	ohm-BREL-loh
Sweater	maglione	mah-LYOH-neh
Scarf	sciarpa	SHAR-pah
Glove	guanto	GWAHN-toh
Hat	cappello	cahp-PEL-loh
Cap	berretto	bear-RET-toh
Underwear	biancheria intima	bee-ahn-care-EE-ah EEN-tee-mah

* Chapter 8 *
Trentino Train Trouble

"It was the train! And two cats have been reported missing." Poni had the satellite phone tight to her right ear. She was waving her left arm wildly. And shouting over the sound of screeching tires and reversed thrusters as *The Flying Pig Machine* touched down at the Bolzano airport. Cincinnati had to hit the brakes hard and reverse the little jet's engines at almost full throttle to stop the plane on the short runway.

"What? We couldn't hear you, *tenente*. What were you shouting?" Césare's voice suddenly boomed out as the plane rolled to a stop and turned slowly left onto a taxiway.

"The smoke. And the ambu-
lances and fire trucks, Césare.
The train has wrecked. Both
owls have escaped. And
two cats have already
been reported missing."
Tenente Poni repeated the
news she'd just learned

from the Interpol agents flying above a train wreck just north of Trento.

"*Santa María. Per l'amor di Dio!*"[1] Césare blurted out. "How could this have happened? Are our agents on the train OK?"

"Quiet just a minute, *per favore*,[2] Césare. Let me hear what the agents in the helicopter are trying to tell me over the noise of their engines," Poni said. She was still waving her arm wildly. This time to ask for quiet. And a minute to hear the rest of what the airborne Interpol agent on the other end of the satellite phone was telling her.

Four pairs of eyes on four unbelieving faces in the cabin glued on her as she listened.

Dusty had taken over taxiing duties. She was heading the sleek little jet to a parking ramp next to the terminal. Cincinnati, not knowing what the others had just heard, strolled back. He had a big smile on his face as he looked at his watch and proclaimed., "Five minutes after nine A.M. We have almost two hours to get to the station and take up our positions." Then he saw the panic written on the faces staring at Poni. And he froze. He seemed to know not to ask any questions. Just to stay quiet so Poni could hear.

As Dusty parked *The Flying Pig Machine* and shut down the engines, Cincinnati leaned in close to Buzz and whispered, "I'll set the wheel chocks. You bring everybody into the terminal. We'll find a quiet corner so I can hear what's going on. From the looks on your faces, I'd guess it isn't good." With that, he turned, pulled down the lever to open the front door and skipped down the steps. He opened a small door under the

---

1. "Saint Mary. For the love of God!"
2. please

wing and pulled out some chained-together wooden blocks shaped like triangles. He started to put them under the plane's two sets of main wheels.

"OK. Thank you, Franco. Stay safe. I'll call you back in fifteen or twenty minutes. Just as soon as we can get a 'plan B' working." Poni closed the little phone and looked up. Her face, too, was troubled. "Let's find *il maialino danzatore*[3] and go inside the terminal. I have a pretty good fix on what just happened," she said softly. "It is truly *incredibile.*"[4]

Dusty stepped out of the cockpit. She still didn't know anything was wrong. "Good flying, Dusty," Buzzer complimented her so everyone could hear. He had picked up that she was troubled somehow when Poni was around.

Dusty smiled at her big brother. She often gave him fits. But she truly loved him. He al-

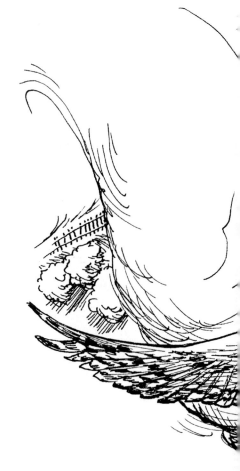

3. the dancing pig
4. incredible, unbelievable

ways seemed to know when she was down. And to find a way to make her feel better.

"We're all going in the terminal to meet some place quiet, Dusty. Poni has some news that must be terrible." Luisa spoke the facts she knew. Even though the mention of Poni having info the rest didn't yet know about might send Dusty Louise back into a funk. She looked at Luigi, who had raised his eyebrows as if to question her judgment. "Luigi, somebody had to tell her what's going on. It might as well be me. I'm already not one of her favorite little sisters, you know."

"You're her only little sister, Luisa." Luigi looked confused. He tried to smile, but his face just wouldn't bend right.

"Very unusual for Luigi," Luisa thought. Then she had another idea. "Luigi," she said, "let's you and I go get everybody a cup of coffee. We can have an *aranciata*. I might even find you some *arachidi con sale*.[5] How'd you like that, *fratello*?"[6]

A big Esso truck had pulled up under the Sabreliner's left wing. Two guys in coveralls were pulling out hoses, getting ready to top off the plane's fuel tanks. Cincinnati called out to them, "Give us a full load. We may be leaving quickly." He thought to himself, "Even though I don't have a clue why. Or where we might go."

Luigi, beaming now at Luisa's mention of salted peanuts, and his tiny twin sister made a beeline for the little *trattoria*[7] in the terminal building as Buzzer and the rest of the group asked to use a private conference room. And were led to it by the airport manager.

---

5. salted peanuts (Luigi's favorite food)
6. brother
7. small restaurant

Dusty, if she was upset with what Luisa had told her, was still thinking, anyway. She asked Buzzer to help her remember to tell the traffic controller in the tower what had caused the smoke north of Trento. "If we find out before he does," she said innocently.

Buzzer turned to the airport manager and whispered something to him. The man's reaction told Dusty that Buzz knew something he hadn't told her yet. "What is it, Buzz? What did you tell him?" Dusty was insistent.

"The smoke, Dusty," he said. "It was from a train wreck. The train we're here to meet. It crashed just north of Trento. That's all I know right now. Poni has talked to the Interpol agents on the scene. We're going now to a conference room where it's quiet. So she can tell us what she learned from a phone call to the Interpol helicopter."

Dusty was stunned. "Why am I always last to know? Huh? Why, Buzzer? You just tell me that!"

"Because we just heard it as you and Cincinnati landed the plane. And Poni was busy getting a report on the phone while you parked the plane. You know everything anybody knows. That's why." Buzzer had an edge to his voice that told Dusty she was about to go too far. "Any more questions?" he asked her sharply.

"No, Buzzy. Sorry." She thought to herself, "I've got to get over this Poni thing. It's ruining my whole trip. This is Italy, for heaven's sake. I ought to be enjoying myself." Then another thought crept into her head. "Why couldn't that Poni have been old? And ugly? Hair falling out? And toothless? Rats!" She smiled at her vision of a truly wretched looking Poni. "I'd like to give her a total makeover," she thought. "Ha!"

The airport manager unlocked a door, opened it and flipped on a light switch. "Here. Use this room as long as you need, *amici*."[8] He looked at Buzzer, adding, "I'll tell the tower what you said. If they get more information on the news ticker, would you like me to bring it to you, *signor gatto smoking*?"[9] he asked.

"Thank you. That would be great," Buzzer responded. Just then Luigi and Luisa appeared with five cups of *espresso*[10], *aranciata* for themselves and an enormous bag of *arachidi con sale*[11] for Luigi. Peanuts in hand, Luigi was quickly returning to his normal mischievous self.

As the owl-chasers took chairs around a small table, all eyes were on *Tenente* Poni.

Césare carefully removed his jaunty yellow straw fedora and placed it on the table in front of him—a sure sign of big trouble, as only Poni knew. He was about to be very serious. "*Tenente Poinsettia Fiore DeVille* has some unsettling news for us," he began.

Poni sat bolt upright. When Césare called her by her entire—and entirely too long, she often thought—name, he expected nothing but total effort. From her. And everyone within earshot. "He might be a little loosey-goosey most of the time," she thought to herself. "But when he takes off that yellow hat and starts calling me *Poinsettia* . . . well, he is the boss."

---

8. friends
9. mister tuxedo cat
10. strong, dark Italian coffee
11. salted peanuts

"Poinsettia, tell us what you know. *Svelto, per favore, tenente. Presto!*"[12]

"Here is the latest information. As of five minutes ago. From Franco, one of our agents in the helicopter." She sipped her espresso. And began to tick off facts.

- 🐾 "The wreck happened at 8:40 A.M. About ten minutes after the train left Trento.
- 🐾 "Both Fred-X and Frieda-K were on the train when it left the Trento station.
- 🐾 "The wreck was thought to have been caused by someone pulling the 'emergency stop' cord as the train went into a sharp curve. You can just imagine who might have done that. Right?
- 🐾 "A fire was deliberately set to burn diesel fuel. That was the black smoke we saw.
- 🐾 "There were only a few minor injuries. Nothing serious. But in the confusion, our onboard agents lost sight of the two owls for only a moment. All agents are unhurt.
- 🐾 "Within a few minutes, the *municipio*[13] in Moena, a small town nearby, reported their two house cats missing. An employee, a *signor Mano di Legno*[14] claims to have seen big birds swoop down and grab the cats. Sound familiar?

"That's all the information I have at the moment. Except our helicopter reported the smoke was so thick they didn't see

---

12. Quickly, please leiutenant. Hurry!
13. local government offices, like a 'city hall'
14. Mister Wooden Hand

any big birds flying away from the scene. They're on the way to Moena right now to talk to this *signor Mano di Legno.*

"That's it, Césare. My guess is the owls pulled the emergency cord, set a diesel fuel fire, and lit out to steal some cats. We have what we think is a *vero*[15] sighting a few kilometers from the wreck site. We do have telephone contact with both the helicopter and the agents on the ground at the wreck site. What do you want to do now?"

Césare didn't hesitate. "Contact *Franco* in the helicopter. Tell him once they talk to this wooden handed guy in Moena, to come directly here. Call us with a report of the witness on the way here. You call our agents on the ground at the train wreck. Tell them we're not in the business of investigating train wrecks. Get the local authorities to give them a ride here.

---

15. accurate, true

"I want all eight agents and that *elicottero francese qui presto, immediatamente!*"[16] While we wait, Buzzer Louis and Cincinnati the dancing pig will come up with what we should do next. They know Fred-X better than anyone." Césare turned to Buzzer and Cincinnati as if to say, "It's all yours. Go for it."

Buzzer looked at Cincinnati. He smiled.

Cincinnati smiled back.

They seemed to be saying, "Let the games begin." Secretly,

each was a little pleased with the sudden turn of events. Just grabbing Fred-X in the Bolzano train station would have been fine. But not very challenging. Now the big bird and his accomplice Frieda-K—who had apparently just committed a crime, herself—were on the loose. And the world now *really*

---

16. French helicopter here quickly, immediately!

needed Sir Buzzer Louis, crime fighting tuxedo cat, and his clever sidekick Cincinnati the dancing pig.

"We're on, Cincinnati!" Buzzer laughed. "So let's get to it."

Do you think Fred-X and Frieda-K really caused the train wreck? Did they escape to Moena and grab the two cats at city hall? Or is this signor Mano di Legno just a timely crackpot? And how do you think Buzzer and Cincinnati will bring Fred-X to justice this time?

Impariamo un po' d'Italiano.

(We're Going to Learn a Little Italian.)

By Luisa Manicotti Giaccomazza

What if you were in Italy and you got ill? Or hurt? And had to go to the doctor—il dottore? Or the drug store— la farmacia? How would you describe what was wrong? Here are a few names of parts of your body to help you.

In English	In Italian	Say It Like This
Ankle	*caviglia*	cah-VEE-lyah
Arm	*braccio*	BRAH-choh
Cheek	*guancia*	GWAHN-chah
Chin	*mento*	MEN-toh
Face	*viso*	VEE-soh
Finger	*dito*	DEE-toh
Hair	*capelli*	cah-PEL-lee
Hand	*mano*	MAH-noh
Head	*testa*	TESS-tah
Hip	*anca*	AHN-cah
Leg	*gamba*	GAHM-bah
Lip	*labbro*	LAHB-broh
Mouth	*bocca*	BOKE-cah
Neck	*collo*	COHL-loh
Shoulder	*spalla*	SPAHL-lah
Stomach	*stomaco*	STOH-mah-coh
Teeth	*dente*	DEN-teh
Toe	*dito del piede*	DEE-toh dell pee-AY-dee
Tongue	*lingua*	LEEN-gwah
Wrist	*polso*	POHL-soh

Part Three

Let the Games Begin

"Maybe I can help Buzzer and Cincinnati now that
Fred-X has flown the coop. For sure I can
figure out how to deal with that Italian
*pomodoro,** Tenente* Poni. Ha!."

—Dusty Louise, the pretty—
and petty—sister

---

* tomato

* Chapter 9 *
Think Evil Thoughts

Bolzano Airport

I miei gemelli[1] had seen a poster in the airport's *trattoria*[2] about a special exhibit at a museum in downtown Bolzano. An exhibit of a man who'd been found a few years before near the Austrian border. Seems he had been frozen in a solid block of ice in the mountains. For more than 5,000 years! Some archaeologists had discovered him. And the local museum had built an ice-cold home for him so visitors could see what people looked—and dressed—like so many years ago. Luigi and Luisa had begged to go see him, putting up quite a fuss. A fuss that was sure to distract from the serious discussion Buzz and Cincinnati needed to have with Césare and Poni. A very private discussion before the other Interpol agents arrived from the train wreck and from talking to *signor Mano di Legno*. The man with the wooden hand from Moena.

---

1. the kitten twins
2. small and informal restaurant

Buzzer had asked Dusty Louise to take the twins to see the 5,000-year-old man in the museum. Dusty wasn't thrilled about it. She didn't want to miss a serious planning meeting. "Dusty, you know that Cincinnati and I need to talk with Césare and Poni, don't you?" Buzz had asked, adding, "I promise you we're not going to do any serious planning until the other agents get here. And you and Luigi and Luisa will be back by then.

"Please do this for me. Thank you, Dusty."

Dusty knew instantly what Buzzer and Cincinnati were going to say to Césare and Poni. She didn't need to hear it. Besides, a trip to the museum with the twins would give her a chance to get away from having to look at that *tenente* for a couple of hours. So she headed off for the museum in a taxi with Luigi and Luisa in tow. "Maybe an old frozen man will help me figure out how to deal with Poni," she thought. "And I'm bound to be the prettiest cat at the museum!"

Back in the airport conference room, with Dusty and the twins sent on their way for a while, Buzzer leaned back in his chair and tried to look relaxed. He spoke directly to Césare. "No, I'm not a bit surprised by what's happened this morning, *signore*[3]. And neither is Cincinnati. Right, *amico*?"[4] He turned and looked at his friend the dancing pig.

---

3. sir
4. friend

Cincinnati spoke softly. "No, Buzzer. I think something strange like this could have been expected."

Césare looked a bit confused. "Why do the two of you say these things?" he asked. "We had everything taken care of. The owls were surrounded. I had eight agents watching them every minute. All the way from Rome. We had a classic arrest all but done. How can you say you're not surprised?"

Buzzer looked at Cincinnati. He smiled. Cincinnati grinned back. "You tell them, Buzzer," the dancing pig said.

"Because, Césare and *tenente*, we've spent a lot of time tracking and capturing Fred-X. You'll never catch him by doing what police everywhere always do. What you would do to catch almost any other criminal just won't work to catch Fred-X. He may be stupid . . ."

"He is stupid, Buzzer. No doubt about it," Cincinnati interrupted.

"Ah, yes, my dancing friend," Buzzer said. "He's stupid, but he is also clever. Very clever. At least when it comes to slipping away. Again and again we've seen it.

"No, my friends, to catch Fred-X will require an unusual plan. A diabolical plan that must be put together in a most unusual way. We must not think like *la polizia*[5]. We must think in a way that is hard for us. But easy for Fred-X."

"And how would that be, Buzzer Louis?" *Tenente* Poni wanted to know.

Buzzer glanced again at Cincinnati. They both leaned across the table. Buzzer Louis almost whispered the answer.

---

5. police

"We must become criminals. Stupid criminals. But clever criminals. Criminals who steal cats. Lots of cats. Criminals who fly those cats away to sell them as slaves. We must become Fred-X in our heads. We must think evil thoughts, *tenente*."

✻   ✻   ✻

Il Museo Municipale in Bolzano[6]

"No, Luigi, I don't want to look at him again. I've seen him twice already. He's all shriveled up. And his clothes are ragged. He looks uncomfortable and miserable. And he's tiny. Yuck!" Luisa had been surprised when she saw the little frozen figure called *l' uomo di ghiaccio*[7].

It seemed to her that Luigi, on the other hand, would stand and look at the ice man all day if the museum's guards didn't tell him over and over to "move along" so others could see, too. Shooed away from the window in front of the exhibit, Luigi ran excitedly to the end of the line so he could pass by again. And again. And again.

Dusty was trying to hurry the little *mici* along. "We need to be heading back to the airport real soon," she said to them as Luigi scampered to the end of the line for one more peek at the frozen old man. "We want to be there when the Interpol agents from Moena and the train wreck get there. I don't want to miss the real planning, you know." She was talking only to Luisa now. Luigi was still in line. "You go tell him, Luisa," Dusty continued. "Tell him this is the last time. No more. And tell him Dusty Louise really means it."

---

6. The City Museum in Bolzano
7. the ice man

* Think Evil Thoughts *

Dusty continued talking to Luisa, who was just standing still, looking at her big sister, "Buzzer said all the right things to get me to bring you two little scamps to the museum. But he forgot to tell Luigi he'd better mind me and be good. Rats! I should have thought of that. I've got to quit thinking about that *tenente*. She's causing me to forget what's important. Especially with you two little *gemelli*."[8]

Luisa smiled and thought to herself, "I might as well say it." Looking up at Dusty, she put on a solemn face and said what she thought needed to be said. "Dusty Louise, what are you talking about? *Tenente* Poni hasn't done anything to you. You're not a victim. Except maybe of your own imagination. Get a life!"

There! She'd said it. Dusty's cheeks puffed out and her eyes began to twitch. "You, little missy, you go get Luigi. *Subito!*[9] We're leaving. And keep your opinions to yourself in the future!"

As Dusty and Luisa were dragging Luigi away from *l' uomo di ghiaccio* and into a taxi to head back to the airport, a black-and-white *Alfa Romeo*[10] sedan of the *carabinieri*[11] pulled up to the Bolzano airport terminal. The four train-riding Interpol agents had arrived.

A big green twin-engine Aerospatiale helicopter was landing and parking next to *The Flying Pig Machine* outside the terminal, too. The flying Interpol agents were there. And they had brought with them a very confused-looking man in a beautiful uniform that seemed like it might belong on a Russian air force general.

---

8. twins
9. Hurry!

10. an Italian-made car
11. Italian state police agency

Buzzer and Cincinnati were watching out the window of the conference room. *"Tenente,* would you meet the agents the *carabinieri* just dropped off, please? Take them to the *trattoria* and get them some lunch. It looks like the helicopter agents might just have brought that *signor Mano di Legno* with them from, where was it? *Moena?*[12] Yes, Moena. I want to talk to him. Césare, would you bring him in here? And send your flying agents to lunch with the others, please? Maybe Poni can debrief all eight agents while we talk to the man from Moena."

What do you think Buzzer wants to talk to *signor Mano di Legno about?* And why does he want the Interpol agents except Césare and Poni to stay out of that meeting? Will Dusty and the twins get back from the museum in time for the real planning? Do you think Luisa's remarks to Dusty will help her? Or just make her madder? And more confused?

---

12. a small town in the Dolomite mountains

Impariamo un po' d'Italiano.

(We're Going to Learn a Little Italian.)

By Luisa Manicotti Giaccomazza

We have seen that the Italian word for 'cousin' is cugino. What about other members of your family? What would you call them if you were in Italy?

In English	In Italian	Say It Like This
Aunt	zia	ZEE-ah
Brother	fratello	frah-TEL-loh
Male cousin	cugino	coo-GEE-noh
Female cousin	cugina	coo-GEE-nah
Daughter	figlia	FEE-lya
Family	famiglia	fah-MEE-lyah
Father	padre	PAH-dreh
Granddaughter	nipotina	nee-poh-TEE-nah
Grandfather	nonno	NOH-noh
Grandmother	nonna	NOH-nah
Grandson	nipotino	nee-poh-TEE-noh
Mother	mamma	MAH-mah
Nephew	nipote	nee-POH-teh
Niece	nipote	nee-POH-teh
Parents	genitori	gen-ee-TOHR-ee
Sister	sorella	sohr-EL-lah
Son	figlio	FEE-lyoh
Uncle	zio	ZEE-oh

✻ Chapter 10 ✻
The Man with
a Wooden Hand

Césare left the conference room to find the man from Moena—the man with the wooden hand and the elegant uniform. Cincinnati the dancing pig was on the little satellite phone talking to Dr. Buford Lewis, Ph.D., and his very smart brother, Bogart-BOGART. Back at the little ranch in the Texas hill country.

"So you see, Dr. Buford and Bogart-BOGART, those owls staged a train wreck this morning. They set fire to some diesel fuel and escaped in the chaos. Does that surprise you?"

"Not really, Cincinnati," Dr. Buford answered. "Bogart-BOGART told me today that the train would never get to Bolzano. Or if it did, those owls wouldn't be on it. Césare's plan just didn't take into account how clever that stupid evil owl can be. Especially when he's threatened."

"So we're going to be coming up with 'plan B,'" Cincinnati said. "It has to be much trickier than a normal police plan, don't you see? Buzzer asked me to fill you in on the details and ask you two to be thinking about how we can grab those owls. Before they grab more Italian cats."

"Here's a clue, Cincinnati." It was Bogart-BOGART now on the line. "There are eight Interpol agents having lunch now. Right?"

"That's right, Bogart-BOGART," Cincinnati answered.

"Think 'duck hunting,' Cincinnati," Bogart-BOGART said, a little mysteriously. "Eight little painted wooden ducks."

Cincinnati smiled. "Exactly where Buzzer and I were headed, Bogart-BOGART. Good thinking. We'll call you back once the plan is set. Do you mind if we wake you up? It might be the middle of the night there in the hills. It's noon here right now."

"*Non c'é problema,* Cincinnati. *Telefonaci. Allora, ciao.*"[1]

As Cincinnati closed the cover of the satellite phone, he marveled at Dr. Buford's younger brother. "Bogart-BOGART really is smart," he thought. "He not only seems to have good owl-catching ideas, but I think he just spoke Italian. *Mamma mia!*"

Buzzer and Poni, who had left the eight agents to eat their lunches, were munching on *panini*[2] from the airport's little *trattoria*. Cincinnati joined them as Césare came into the room with *ancora due panini*[3] and the man who must be *signor Mano di Legno*.

"Buzzer Louis, *Tenente* Poni and Cincinnati the dancing pig, *le presento il signor Mano di Legno da Moena.*[4] *Questo signore*[5]

---

1. "No problem. Call us. Goodbye, now."
2. sandwiches
3. two more sandwiches
4. "I present to you Mr. Wooden Hand from Moena."
5. This gentleman

believes he saw Fred-X and Frieda-K steal two cats in his village. And fly away with them."

Buzzer put down his sandwich. And swallowed. "Thank you, *signore*, for coming to see us. Tell us please exactly what you saw this morning." Buzzer smiled.

Césare answered for the man with the wooden hand while Poni translated Buzz's question. "The *signore* does not speak *inglese*,[6] Buzzer. He wants to know if either of you speak German. I've told him only Luigi and Luisa speak *italiano*."

"In fact, I do speak German, Césare. But Buzzer doesn't. He speaks Russian and two Chinese languages. But not German. Look, Césare, this is going to get too confusing. And take too long. Why not just let the *tenente* translate from Italian to English. Let's keep it simple. And short. If we can," Cincinnati suggested.

"I can help, too." It was Luisa. She and Dusty and Luigi had hurried into the room while Cincinnati was talking.

"*Sí, sí*, Césare. Luisa *ed io*,[7] we can translate." Poni looked at the two kittens and added, "And Luigi, *anche*,[8] if we get stuck."

Luigi looked at the *tenente* and beamed.

Dusty looked at her, too, with a mixture of disgust and confusion. And thought to herself, "She's really something. Cozying up to Luigi like that. She knows I can't speak Italian. But," she thought with a wisp of a smile, "she can't speak Spanish!"

Buzzer, as though reading Dusty's mind, shot her a stern glance. "Finally!" Luisa thought. "Buzzer's finally noticing how Dusty's acting when Poni's around. Good!"

---

6. English
7. "Yes, yes, Césare. Luisa and I."
8. too

"Good idea, Cincinnati," Césare said. "Poni and Luisa will translate. English to Italian. And Italian to English." He looked across the room and quickly added, "And Luigi, too."

"OK, let's start over. Poni and Luisa, please ask Mr. Wooden Hand to tell us exactly what he saw this morning," Buzzer said.

Poni spoke to the man from Moena. Luisa chipped in a word and a phrase. While he was answering their question, Buzzer leaned over to Dusty. "Dusty Louise, you're a beautiful cat. The prettiest gray tabby I've ever seen. Poni's pretty, too. But she's a calico. You do not have to compete with her. Besides, she can't fly an airplane. And I'll bet she can't speak Spanish, either. Each of you has your own talents. And both of you are beautiful. So stop it, do you hear me? Stop comparing yourself to her. And her to you. You're acting ridiculous!"

Dusty started to pout. Then she smiled, just a little. "Thank you, Buzzer. I'll try."

Luisa, noticing the exchange between her big brother and sister, leaned over to Luigi, who'd just come up with the Italian word for 'house-cat' and whispered, "Buzz's on the job. This business between Dusty and Poni is about to come to a screeching halt. *Finito!*"[9]

Signor Mano di Legno finished speaking. He sat with his hands folded, looking a bit confused.

Tenente Poni looked around the room. "Here's what *il signore* has told us," she began. "He started by wanting to know if he's in any trouble. I told him 'no,' that we are grateful for his help. And we will return him to Moena very quickly. He was

---

9. Finished!

Signor Mno di Legno.

working at his job this morning in the *municipio*[10] in Moena. He takes care of two cats who live there. And he delivers packages and messages to and from the *municipio*. That's his job. At about ten minutes before nine o'clock this morning, he was returning from *l'ufficio postale*—the post office, I believe you would call it. He had taken some mail to be sent to Trento from the *municipio*. Mostly from the *geometra*[11] office. *Come si dice 'geometra' in inglese, Luisa¿"*[12]

"Io non capisco 'geometra,'[13] Poni. Luigi¿"

"'Surveyor' is the word in English, I believe." Luigi was proud. He not only was paying attention, but he also had actually been helpful. *"Buon lavoro, signor Luigi, il gatto magnifico,"*[14] he thought to himself.

"Yes, *sí*. Mostly from the surveyor's office," the *tenente* continued her report. "He says he was walking down *il marciapiede*,[15] uh, the sidewalk, no, Luisa¿" Luisa nodded yes. "He was walking down the sidewalk toward the *municipio* when he saw two big birds in the morning sky. He says they were coming from the southwest. And they were flying frantically. Well, they swooped right over his head. Not a meter from him. He felt the wind—*il vento*—from them as they sped by.

"He said he was astonished. Not only because they were flying so fast and looked so frantic, but also because they swooped right into the front door of the *municipio*. He began

---

10. city hall
11. surveyor
12. "How do you say 'geometra' in English, Luisa?"
13. I don't know 'geometra'
14. "Good work, Mr. Luigi, the magnificent cat."
15. the sidewalk

to run to the building. But just before he got there, he says, out they came again. Fast and furious.

"Only this time they seemed to each have a cat with them. Carrying it by their talons. '*O, Santa María,*'[16] he thought to himself, 'what's going on here?'

"And then the birds disappeared. They were heading northeast toward the *Marmolada e Cortina d'Ampezzo.*"[17]

"What happened then? What did he do?" Dusty Louise seemed to be returning to her usual impatient self.

"He rushed into the city hall to find his cats—the two he takes care of. The ones who live in the building. But they weren't there. Gone. Nowhere to be found. Then, he said, he was sure the big birds had stolen them away. That's when he called the *carabinieri*[18] in Trento to report them catnapped," Poni seemed to have finished.

Signor Mano di Legno spoke. "*Ci sono domande?*"[19] he asked.

"He asks if there are any questions," Luigi piped up.

"Yes. Please ask him to tell us what these two missing cats look like, *tenente,*" Buzzer said.

Poni spoke a few words and the *signore* from Moena responded.

"He says they both look exactly like Luigi and Luisa. Only

16. 'Oh, Saint Mary'
17. famous mountain and town in Italy
18. state police
19. "Are there questions?"

just a little bigger. They're still kittens, it seems." Poni translated the descriptions.

"I'll put out an APB—All Points Bulletin—at once," Césare started to get up.

"No, please, Césare. We must not involve too many authorities. Remember, Fred-X may be stupid, but he's clever. If we get all the *poliziotti*[20] in Italy involved, he'll just slip away from us again. And again. He's done the same thing before. In Mexico. He nabbed two gourds from the top of a tall pine tree. He thought they were Luigi and Luisa. That's how we trapped him. My bet is he's going to grab every little orange tabby he sees. For the rest of his life. Think so, Cincinnati?"

"Very likely, Buzzer. When those two furry little creatures in Mexico turned out to be gourds and not Luigi and Luisa, he was struck dumb. They made an impression on him. For sure."

Césare looked around the room. "Before we take *signor Mano di Legno* home, are there any other questions?"

Luigi waved his paw frantically.

"Luigi, you have a question for the *signore*?" Césare asked.

"Yes. I'd really like to know how he got that neat hand made of wood. What happened? Is that okay to ask, Buzzer?"

Luigi turned to look at his big brother as Luisa held her breath.

"I don't know, Luigi. What do you think, *tenente*?" Buzzer shifted the question to the translator.

"It will be fine to ask. As long as we don't insist, Luigi," Poni said. "He may not wish to talk about it. Since it has

---

20. policemen

nothing to do with catching owls, we can only ask. Politely. All right, Césare?" she asked her boss.

"Sure. Why not? Maybe he's a hero of some kind. *Chi lo sa?*"[21]

Poni smiled at *signor Mano di Legno* and politely asked him a question. To everyone's relief, he smiled back at her and spoke a few sentences in Italian.

"He says he was a young boy after World War II. In Moena. He and some of his friends found a German land mine in a riverbed. Before they knew what happened, the mine exploded and tore off his left hand. So he has a wooden hand and wears a glove of the finest *pelle*[22] to cover it. It's a sad story, but he is proud of it. The hand, that is," Poni looked at Luigi.

Signor Mano di Legno looked at him too. Luigi smiled and blurted out in Italian. "*É una mano squisita, signore. Mi piace molto.*"[23]

"*Grazie, micio,*" the *signore* responded. "*Sei un gattito squisito, anche tu.*"[24]

"I guess that was a good question after all, Luigi," Luisa said. "I never would have asked it. Even though we were all dying to know the answer. But it seems like he didn't mind. Score one more for the Luigi-ster," she laughed.

"If there are no more questions, Césare, do you think we can ask the *carabinieri* to return *signor Mano di Legno* to Moena? We have a serious owl-catching plan to get to. And I'd like your agents to be here when we're finished." Buzzer had

---

21. Who knows?
22. leather
23. "It's a fine hand, sir. I like it a lot."
24. "Thank you, kitten. You are a fine little cat, too."

been thinking. Cincinnati had, too. They were ready to hatch "plan B," a most diabolical plot to do in Fred-X and his evil ways.

For the last time.

Do you think Fred-X and Frieda-K might believe they've captured Luigi and Luisa? Or are they just going to grab every small orange tabby they see? Where do you think they're headed with *signor Mano di Legno*'s cats from Moena? And what will Buzzer and Cincinnati's new plan have to do with duck hunting?

Impariamo un po' d'Italiano.

(We're Going to Learn a Little Italian.)

By Luisa Manicotti Giaccomazza

What if you wanted to talk about sports with someone who only speaks Italian? What would you call the names of the games? Here are a few to help you.

In English	In Italian	Say It Like This
Auto racing	*automobile da corsa*	ah-oo-toh-moh-BEE-leh dah COHR-sah
Baseball	*baseball*	BAH-seh-bahl
Basketball	*pallacanestro*	pahl-lah-cah-NES-troh
Cycling	*ciclismo*	chee-CLEESE-moh
Fishing	*pesca*	PES-cah
Football	*pallone*	pahl-LOH-neh
Gymnastics	*ginnastica*	geen-NAHS-tee-cah
Hockey	*hockey*	OH-key
Running	*corsa*	COHR-sah
Sailing	*vela*	VAY-lah
Skiing	*corse con gli sci*	COHR-seh COHN lyee SHEE
Soccer	*calcio*	CAHL-choh
Swimming	*nuoto*	Noo-OH-toh
Tennis	*tennis*	TEHN-nees
Volleyball	*palla a volo*	pahl-lah ah VOH-loh

* Chapter 11 *
Plan B ... Hunting Ducks

"So, Buzzer and Cincinnati, you've come up with a new plan for capturing Fred-X, huh? 'Plan B'? Tell us about it. Is it truly—what is the word you used? Diabolical?" Césare asked. He picked up his jaunty yellow straw fedora and shoved it down hard on his head. A sure sign, according to *Tenente* Poni, that he was ready to "get on with it." Whatever "it" might be. "Maybe the *tenente* and I will learn something new to help us in the future, no?"

Buzzer wasn't sure if Césare was being sarcastic since his own plan had failed. Or if he really might be open to finding new ways to capture evildoers.

The four cats from Texas, Cincinnati the dancing pig, Césare and the *tenente* all sat around the conference room table at the Bolzano airport. *Signor Mano di Legno* had been sent back to Moena with the *carabinieri* in their black-and-white *Alfa Romeo*. And the eight Interpol agents who'd tracked the ill-fated train throughout last night had gone to a nearby hotel to get some sleep. "A few winks, at least," Césare had told them.

Luigi and Luisa sat slumped in their chairs. After their morning at the *museo*, a *panino* each for lunch and some non-stop snacking on Luigi's big bag of *arachidi con sale*, both were sleepy. They might be able to stay awake to hear about the new plan. Or they might not.

Buzzer sat back in his chair. He motioned to Cincinnati to start talking about what they were all now calling "plan B."

Cincinnati leaned forward and spoke softly. "This 'plan B,' Césare and *tenente*, began to form even before we got to Rome. It is important, as I'm sure you know, to always be ready just in case something goes haywire." Césare looked confused. Poni turned to Luisa and held out both palms as if to say, "I don't understand."

Luisa interrupted. "Cincinnati, I think they don't understand the word 'haywire.'" She looked at Poni. "It means 'to go wrong,' I think. That would be a good way to say it. 'In case something goes wrong.'"

"Sorry," Cincinnati apologized. "I'll try not to use confusing words." He went on, "The idea of a different plan was taking shape in our talks even as Fred-X and Frieda-K got on the train to Bolzano. Buzzer and I, as we've told you, had doubts that the train would ever get to Bolzano. Or, if it did, that the two big birds would still be on it. So we began to think and talk about other ways to capture the *due gufi giganti*."[1] He looked to Luisa to be sure he had used the right Italian words. She nodded yes.

---

1. two giant owls

* Plan B ... Hunting Ducks *

"So we were plotting and planning all along. Just in case. It was in a phone call an hour or two ago that a flash of the blindingly obvious hit me, though."

Again, Césare and the *tenente* looked to Luisa. "'A flash of the blindingly obvious' tells about something so simple that it has been overlooked. Right, Cincinnati?" Luisa offered.

"Yes, Luisa. I was talking to Dr. Buford Lewis and his very smart brother Bogart-BOGART. They often have helped us think about clever ways to do in bad guys. Well, Bogart-BOGART offered what he called a 'clue' to capturing Fred-X once again. He said, 'Think about duck hunting.' And the light went on in my head."

Cincinnati, realizing he had once again used a phrase peculiar to English as it's spoken in *Stati Uniti*,[2] quickly added, "I understood at once how we should go about catching those catnabbing owls this time."

"So, what is 'plan B?'" Dusty, as usual impatient to get to the answer, wanted to know.

Buzzer stepped in to take the floor and begin to answer Dusty's—and everyone's—questions. Cincinnati smiled and sat back.

"A good plan," Buzzer began, "a clever plan that has a chance of working cannot just be told. No, a truly diabolical plan must be discovered. Step by step. I'll try to tell you in small steps, then, what Cincinnati and I are suggesting we do. And if I am successful, you'll each discover the plan. And the genius of the plan. For yourselves. OK?"

"Fair enough, Buzzer," Césare said. "Go ahead, *per favore*."[3]

---

2. United States   3. please

"I'll begin with a question. Just to get everyone thinking. And to keep Luigi awake." He winked at his tiny baby brother and smiled. Luigi sprang up. He stood tall and saluted.

"I'm paying attention, *fratello mio. Non ti preoccupare.*"[4]

Buzzer continued. "Here's my question. It's for Césare and Poni. Tell me three things that Italy produces that are the best of their kind? Not best according only to Italians. But known as the best by all the world?"

Césare pushed back the brim of his yellow straw hat. He turned to Poni. They exchanged a few comments that nobody else in the room could hear. He turned back to Buzzer. "The first thing we will name is ice cream, Buzzer. We believe the whole world knows that our *gelato*[5] is simply the best. Nobody makes better ice cream than Italians. Do you agree?"

Buzzer looked at Cincinnati. The dancing pig smiled. And nodded.

"Yes, Césare. We agree. Italian *gelato* is the best ice cream in the world. Nobody makes it better. Now, what's your second choice?" Buzzer asked.

"Can we get some *gelato*, Buzzer. Huh? Pleeez. Right now." Luigi was smacking his lips and pointing in the general direction of the *trattoria*.

As Césare and the *tenente* compared thoughts quietly between themselves, Buzzer gave Luigi fifteen Euros and sent him and Luisa to get seven *gelati*. "A *gelato* right now sounds good to me, too, Luigi. Get us all one. Buy seven different flavors," Buzzer said.

Tenente Poni looked at Buzz and Cincinnati. She was ready

---

4. my brother. Don't worry.   5. ice cream

with their second answer. "We think the world would agree that Italians make the best motorcycles, too," she said. "That's our second choice, Buzzer."

Cincinnati laughed and leaned forward. "Buzzer, this is working. They're getting it," he said.

"Right you are, Poni. A second item is definitely motorcycles. Nobody makes a better cycle than *Motoguzzi*,"[6] Buzzer said. "So that's two. What's your third choice?"

"I don't see what ice cream and motorcycles have to do with catching owls, Buzzer. When is this going to make some sense?" Dusty was getting frustrated with Buzzer and Cincinnati's little riddle. And a game of discovering the plan she was beginning to think was *matto, pazzo*.[7] "When will you get to the point here? Those owls are running amok out there while we're sitting here playing riddles," she said. "Cincinnati started out saying something about duck hunting. I don't see what ice cream and motorcycles have to do with ducks. Or owls. Or hunting either of them. This is so frustrating!" Dusty was wringing her paws. Getting more nervous by the minute.

"Have some *gelato*, Dusty. It'll chill you out." Luigi and Luisa walked in the door carefully carrying a tray. On it were seven bowls of *gelato*. "Here, Dusty, we got you *gelato nocciolino*.[8] And, no, it's not because we think you're a nut. Even though you are. Sometimes. Like right now," Luigi laughed. And everyone in the room laughed with him. Even Dusty Louise, whose favorite ice cream flavor was *nocciolino*. She knew why the twins had gotten her that flavor. And it made

6. Italian brand of expensive motorcycles
7. two words for 'crazy'
8. hazelnut ice cream

her happy that they had remembered. Or even thought about her and what she liked best.

Buzzer resumed control of the meeting as everyone dug into their bowls of *gelato*. "So now we've agreed. Ice cream and motorcycles are two excellent Italian products. What would you say is a third, Césare and Poni?" he asked.

"Shotguns, Buzzer," Césare responded. "Italians make the world's best shotguns. Is that what you had in mind?"

"Exactly!" Buzzer, unlike his normal quiet self, was actually getting a little excited. "Italian shotguns made by the famous Italian gun maker, Césare Guerini. Best in the world.

"And who uses shotguns for sport, I ask you? At least who is one group to whom shotguns are very important?" Not waiting for an answer, Buzzer plunged ahead. "Duck hunters, that's who.

"So there you have it. The three things we can all agree are the best in the world and come from Italy . . . ice cream, motorcycles, and shotguns. These three are the keys to plan B. Now, at last, we must all think evil thoughts. Just like that criminal Fred-X.

"Is everything becoming clear to you yet?," Buzzer continued. "Are you beginning to see the diabolical plan we're hatching here? No? Not yet? Then my friend Cincinnati the dancing pig will explain to you how we'll use the most excellent reputations of all three of these great products to catch that evil pair of owls. And put them out of the cat-nabbing business. Once and for all time."

Buzzer smiled. A dark, almost sinister grin that gave Luisa and Luigi chills just looking at it. Or was it the gelato chilling them?

* Plan B ... Hunting Ducks *

What in the world is Buzzer talking about? How will ice cream, motorcycles and shotguns help our little group catch Fred-X? And what of duck hunters? What do they have to do with anything? Is he talking about duck hunters who ride motorcycles and eat ice cream? And what does all that have to do with catching criminals?

Impariamo un po' d'Italiano.
(We're Going to Learn a Little Italian.)
By Luisa Manicotti Giaccomazza

If you were to travel in Italy, you'd find it important to understand words that tell about the weather. So you would know what to wear. And what to expect when you go outside. Here are some weather words to help you.

In English	In Italian	Say It Like This
Weather	*tempo*	TEM-poh
Climate	*clima*	CLEE-mah
It is hot	*fa caldo*	fah CAHL-doh
It is cold	*fa freddo*	fah FRAY-doh
It is windy	*tira vento*	TEER-ah VEN-toh
Rain	*piove*	pee-OH-veh
It's raining	*sta piovendo*	stah pee-oh-VEHN-doh
Rainy	*piovoso*	pee-oh-VOH-soh
Snow	*neve*	NEH-veh
Clouds	*nuvole*	NOO-voh-leh
Storm	*tempesta*	tem-PESS-tah
Thunder	*tuono*	too-OH-noh
Lightning	*lampo*	LAHM-poh
Hail	*grandine*	grahn-DEE-neh
Temperature	*temperatura*	tem-pear-ah-TOOR-ah
Sun	*sole*	SOH-leh
Sunlight	*luce del sole*	LOO-cheh del SOH-leh
Moon	*luna*	LOO-nah
Moonlight	*chiaro di luna*	kee-AHR-oh dee LOO-nah

* Chapter 12 *
The Bait ...
Eight Little 'Painted Ducks'

Before Cincinnati the dancing pig started his explanation of more of the details of plan B, *Tenente* Poni asked for a short break. She'd been nonstop busy since just before *The Flying Pig Machine* touched down in Bolzano. She needed a few minutes. To gather her thoughts. And maybe to just take a little walk. To clear her head.

During the recess in the meeting, Luigi regaled his cousin Césare with a few too many questions about their grandfather. The one who had been *il marchese di Venezia*.[1] "So, Césare, did you meet *il nonno*?[2] Did you actually get to know him? Tell us about him—Luisa and me. *Per favore.*"

"Luigi and Luisa, yes I did know him. When I was a small kitten like you. And he was a very old cat. *Il nonno Giacomo Spezzatino Giaccomazza* is a national hero in Italy. Did you

---

1. the marquis of Venice   2. grandfather

know that? Yes, *cugini miei,*[3] *il nonno* was a *Garibaldino.*[4] The right hand—and some said the brains—of the famous General Giuseppe Garibaldi. Italy was not a country until just over a hundred years ago. No, it was a loose collection of city-states ruled from the Vatican. They were called 'papal states.' Grandfather Giaccomazza was the marquis of Venice, one of the most powerful of those city-states.

"General Garibaldi united the many city-states into a single country in the 1870s. The unity was led by your grandfather and the Venetians—the people of Venice. A man named Victor Emmanuel was named king. And Italy has been a country separate from the rule of the popes ever since." Césare had the rapt attention of the two little orange tabbies.

"What did he look like, Césare?" Luigi asked.

"Was he nice to you?" Luisa wanted to know.

"He looked exactly like the two of you. He was a bright orange tabby. He was called *il gatto arancione*[5] by the Venetians. They loved him. And, yes Luisa, he was very nice to me. He couldn't see very well. Because he was so old, of course. And he couldn't move around very well, either. But he called me '*mio piccolo Césare*'[6]. He would ask me to read to him. Or tell him what I could see on the bay of Venice as we sat together in the *piazza* in front of St. Mark's cathedral. He had me bring him things. I don't think he really wanted those things. He just wanted to play with me. And keep me busy. I've missed him many times since those days. Especially when I have a reason to visit *Venezia.*[7]

---

3. my cousins
4. grandfather was a follower of Garibaldi

5. the orange cat
6. 'my little Césare.'
7. Venice

"The two of you remind me of him—a great orange tabby. That's why I'm so fond of you, *piccoli cugini*."[8] Césare had finished his story about their grandfather. He sat quietly and stared out the window across the runway toward the mountains that ringed Bolzano.

"Thank you, Césare. It's nice to know more about *il nostro nonno*,"[9] Luisa said.

"Yes, it's nice, all right Césare. No doubt about that. But don't weird-out on us," Luigi said.

---

8. little cousins
9. our grandfather

Luisa shot her little brother a dark glance. But Césare burst into laughter. "You are funny *come il nostro nonno Giaccomazza*,[10] Luigi. He was a very funny cat, too."

"Some day I'll be a national hero of a country, too" Luigi said.

It was Luisa's turn to burst into laughter. "And what country might that be, Luigi?" she asked. "Upper Elbo Macaronia?"

"I think you're funny, too, Luisa," Césare said.

The tiny kittens smiled. They were proud to be like their famous grandfather.

While Cincinnati made some notes to help him explain plan B to the others, Buzzer was on the satellite phone. Making the return call Cincinnati had promised to Dr. Buford Lewis and his very smart brother Bogart-BOGART.

"So our plan B will be built on shotguns, motorcycles, and ice cream," he said to the two Labrador retrievers. Buford and Bogart-BOGART had Buzzer on a speaker phone so both could be in on the conversation. "Can you figure it out, Bogart-BOGART?" Buzzer asked.

"I think I have a pretty good idea, Buzzer," Bogart-BOGART answered.

"Tell me," Buzzer said.

Bogart-BOGART paused. He was thinking.

"Buzzer," he began, "I see an organized hunting trip. And then a really big show for a lot of people. Finally, I think there will be a huge party near some water. Am I close?" the smart Labrador retriever asked.

"I think you have it, Bogart-BOGART. Explain it to Dr. Buford when we hang up. I have to get back to our meeting.

---

10. like our grandfather Giaccomazza

Cincinnati's going to go into the tactics of plan B with César, the *tenente* and my brother and sisters. *Ciao.*"[11]

Buzzer put away the little satellite phone and walked back into the conference room. The group was coming back together.

"Look at that, Luigi!" Luisa almost pointed, but caught herself just in time. Still, her eyes bugged out. Big time.

"Oh my gosh, Luisa," Luigi said. "Dusty's actually talking to *Tenente* Poni."

"What do you suppose that's all about?" Luisa wondered.

"I don't know, Luigi, but they're not hitting each other. Or screaming. No hair pulling. Those are good signs, I think."

The twins passed Dusty Louise and *Tenente* Poni just in time to hear Dusty say, "Yes, Poni, Buzzer does like to be a little mysterious. He plays these mind games with us all the time.

"He says it'll help the twins learn to think. I'm still as confused as you are, *tenente*. But I'll bet I figure it out before you do!"

"Oops. We could have done without that last little comment," Luigi smiled. "No hair pulling yet, Luisa. But I'll bet it's coming."

As they all sat back down around the table, Cincinnati rose to speak.

"Has anybody figured out the details of plan B yet?" he asked.

Buzzer smiled as five pairs of eyes fixed on the dancing pig as if he had just said something truly weird.

"OK, then, I'll begin to reveal a little more of the details. If

---

11. Goodbye

you think you have it figured out, just speak right up. I'll give a ride in that French helicopter out there to the first one who figures it all out.

"So far, we're dealing with ice cream, motorcycles, and shotguns. And maybe duck hunting." Cincinnati paused.

"I have it! I have it! I know what the plan is!" Luigi leaped up on the table and was waving both arms frantically in Cincinnati's direction.

"Really?" Cincinnati said. "OK, Luigi, let's hear it."

"I want to go to Venice!" Luigi was truly excited.

"What? You want to go to Venice? What're you talking about, Luigi?" Cincinnati was amused. But also completely confused.

"In the French helicopter, Cincinnati. Take me to Venice!" To Luigi, everything was perfectly clear. He couldn't see why Cincinnati didn't get it.

"Luigi, you can't claim the prize until you solve the puzzle," the dancing pig said to the little *micio*.[12] "Tell me how plan B works. If you're right, I'll take you to Venice. How's that?" Cincinnati looked at Luigi, waiting for an answer.

"Oh, sorry. I must have missed something," Luigi said. "But can I guess anyway?"

"You get one guess right now, Luigi," Cincinnati said.

"Okay, Cincinnati. Here is plan B. "Buzzer buys Luisa and me both a *Vespa*.[13] We steal a shotgun from Césare. Then we shoot Fred-X. And *Il Papa*[14] gives us a huge bowl of ice cream

___

12. kitten
13. a fast Italian motor scooter. "Vespa" is the Italian word for wasp.
14. the Pope

as a reward. Isn't that right?" Luigi was sure he had it. Well, almost sure.

"Not exactly, Luigi." Buzzer was speaking. And trying not to laugh. "First, Luigi, we're the good guys. We don't steal shotguns. And I hardly think the Pope will reward you for stealing a shotgun and killing an owl. Even an evil owl like Fred-X."

"But you said to think evil thoughts. You said it, Buzzer. You said we have to become like Fred-X in our heads. He steals cats. Doesn't he?"

"Luigi, we must only pretend to be like Fred-X in our heads. To help us catch him. But we never want to act like him," Buzzer smiled at his baby brother.

"However, Luigi, I must tell you," Buzzer went on, "you have come very close to two important parts of plan B. You got them a little cockeyed, but you're on the right track," Buzzer said.

"No prize yet, Luigi." Cincinnati said. "But I like the way you're thinking. Keep it up."

Césare looked at Dusty and the *tenente*. "Luigi's answer makes more sense than anything I've come up with yet. I'm totally stumped. Still ..." he said.

"Shall I go on?" Cincinnati didn't wait for an answer. Or want one.

"Let's take the clues one at a time. Start with shotguns," Cincinnati said. "I'll tell you that we won't really ever need a shotgun. But a duck hunter does. He needs a good shotgun. And what else does he need? Any ideas, Luisa?"

"Warm clothes, rubber boots and maybe some decoys?" Luisa guessed.

"Right!" Cincinnati shouted the word and pointed straight at Luisa. "You said the magic word, Luisa. 'Decoys.' Every duck hunter needs a shotgun, warm clothes. And some decoys. And so do we. Need some decoys. Where can we get them? And what should they look like?"

"Not ducks." Luigi was back in the game.

"I know, Cincinnati," Dusty Louise said. "They should look like cats."

"Right, Dusty. Excellent. Now we're getting somewhere. And where would we find oh, say, maybe as many as eight decoys that look like cats, I wonder?" Cincinnati said.

Tenente Poni suddenly sat bolt upright. "I have them already, Cincinnati," she said. "At the *Albergo Luna*.[15] Right down the road about four kilometers. Getting a wink or two of sleep."

Césare looked at his assistant. "You're talking about our agents?" he asked. "How are they decoys?"

"They're not yet, Césare. But I'll bet they're about to be," Luigi piped up.

"Tell us, Luigi," Cincinnati urged the little kitten to go on.

"We'll use them to lure Fred-X and Frieda-K. Just like decoys," Luigi said. "We'll put them in pairs in all the little towns from here to Venice. Right? And can I go to Venice with them?"

"You're all starting to think. I congratulate you," Buzzer said. "Our first step in plan B is to assign Césare and Poni's agents to small towns around our last sighting of the big birds. That was Moena. Right? So we'll let them sleep for a couple more hours and then move them into position.

---

15. Hotel Moon

"Poni, they're to be very visible. Make a lot of noise and move around a lot. Just be sure if the evil owls are anywhere around they won't miss seeing our decoys. And be sure each has a small two-way radio and cell phone so they can report in. If they're stolen and carried away, we'll want to know where Fred-X and Frieda-K have taken them."

"Where shall we put them, Buzzer?" Césare wanted to know specifics.

"Two in Predazzo. Two in Canazei. Two in San Martino di Castrozza. And two in Cortina d'Ampezzo. I want to talk to them before you move them out, though. Is that OK with you, Césare?" Buzzer asked glancing up from the map he'd been studying.

Césare nodded. "OK with me. It's your show, Buzzer."

"Where are we going to be?" Dusty asked.

"In Moena, Dusty. Right in the middle of the circle," Cincinnati answered.

"Your brother's very clever, Dusty Louise. You must have learned a lot from him." Poni leaned over and spoke directly to Dusty.

"All the Giaccomazzas are clever, *tenente*. Every last one of us," Dusty responded. She bit off each word as if it were on a piece of string cheese.

So we now know about shotguns and duck hunting. But what about ice cream? And motorcycles? Which will be at the heart of the second step of plan B? Is Dusty getting over her jealousy of the *tenente*? Or do you think she'll take every chance to keep making not-too-nice remarks? And when will Luigi get to go to Venice?

Impariamo un po' d'Italiano.

(We're Going to Learn a Little Italian.)
By Luisa Manicotti Giaccomazza

When you eat a meal in Italy, you'll need to know what to call things on the table. Here are a few words to get you started.

In English	In Italian	Say It Like This
Bowl	tazza	TAHTZ-zah
Chair	sedia	SAY-dya
Cup	coppa	COH-pah
Dining room	sala da pranzo	SAH-lah dah PRAHN-zoh
Eat	mangia	MAHN-jah
Fork	forchetta	fohr-KET-tah
Glass	bicchiere	bee-kee-AIR-reh
Kitchen	cucina	coo-CHEE-nah
Knife	coltello	coal-TEL-loh
Napkin	tovagliuolo	toh-vah-Lyoo-OH-loh
Plate	piatto	pee-AHT-toh
Spoon	cucchiaio	coo-CHY-yoh
Table	tavola	TAH-voh-lah
Tablecloth	tovaglia	toh-VAH-lya

* Chapter 13 *
CIA's Angels

"*Qual'è la parola per 'decoy' in italiano? Come si dice decoy, Luisa?*"[1] *Tenente* Poni couldn't think of the Italian word for "decoy."

"*Io penso che la parola è 'esca,' tenente,*"[2] Luisa said.

"*Certo, Luisa. Esca.*"[3] Poni smiled. "It's good to have some help with this business of translating," she thought to herself. "Luisa is a cutie. Luigi, too. I'm not sure about Dusty Louise, though. She seems to have *un' ape nel cappello.*"[4]

Tenente Poni joined Buzzer Louis, Cincinnati and Césare, who were giving the eight "decoy" cat-agents their instructions. Luigi and Luisa headed back to the *trattoria* for another *aranciata.* "*Questi arachidi con sale*[5] sure do make me thirsty," Luigi said.

"Me, too, Luigi," Luisa said. "Of course, we don't have to

---

1. "What's the word for 'decoy' in Italian? How do you say 'decoy?'"
2. "I think the word is 'esca,' lieutenant.
3. "Of course, Luisa. Esca."
4. a bee in her bonnet
5. these salted peanuts

keep eating and eating and eating them, you know. I'll bet you've eaten a quart so far."

"If I'm the big *arachidi* eater, Luisa, how come you've got a ring of salt all around your mouth?" Luigi shot back.

Luisa quickly wiped her mouth on a napkin. "Better?" she asked.

"All gone," Luigi answered.

In the conference room the eight Interpol agents listened carefully as Buzzer gave them their instructions.

"Finally," Buzzer said to them, "don't be afraid. As far as we know, Fred-X has stolen hundreds of cats. Maybe thousands. But he's never hurt any of them, himself. Not one. He once carried me almost six hundred kilometers nonstop. Never hurt me. Not a bit. He's a catnabber. But not a killer. A really strange bird."

"What we want you to do as decoys," Cincinnati spoke up, "is to get captured. Then we suggest you just go limp. As we say in *inglese*, 'play possum.'" Cincinnati looked to Césare to explain what that meant. Césare shrugged. He didn't know either. So the *tenente* tried to explain.

"Pretend to be dead. Or sleeping," she said.

"Thank you, *tenente*," Cincinnati said. He turned to the eight agents. "Your jobs as decoys are very, very important. We want you to get captured. Fly with Fred-X or Frieda-K to see where they're taking all the cats. And then when they leave you all locked up, call Césare or *Tenente* Poni and tell us where you are. No harm will come to you. I promise. On my mammy's hammy." Cincinnati laughed. And when Césare finished translating, so did the cat agents from Interpol. All eight of them.

Césare sent the cat agents off in pairs. Two each to the villages of Canazei, Cortina d'Ampezzo, San Martino di Castrozza, and Predazzo. They left together in the big green Interpol Aerospatiale helicopter.

"Drop them off, *sergente*,"[6] he told the helicopter's pilot, "and then bring that big *elicottero francese*[7] right back here. The rest of us will be ready to go to Moena by then."

I gatti della CIA,[8] Cincinnati, Césare, and the *tenente* gathered again in the conference room. Cincinnati was ready to reveal step two of plan B. The dancing pig stood at the head of the conference table.

"Let's take a look now at step two of our diabolical plan," he said. Cincinnati held up what seemed to be a large piece of paper rolled into a tube. "Remember," he said, "the second step will be about motorcycles. Before I unroll this poster and tape it on the wall, does anybody want to guess how we'll use motorcycles to catch Fred-X and Frieda-K?" he asked.

Luigi jumped up. He seemed to have one thing on his mind. "Buzzer will buy Luisa and me *Vespas*," he said once again. "And we'll race all around. Fred-X and Frieda-K will chase us. We'll go faster and faster. Then we'll run up a long ramp to jump over six buses. As we fly through the air, we'll smack into Fred-X and Frieda-K. That'll knock them to the ground. Then you can grab them and, voilá. The evil owls are captured. How's that?"

Luisa was staring wide-eyed at her little twin brother. "Luigi, have you completely lost it?" she asked. "I'm not

---

6. sergeant
7. French helicopter
8. The cats of the CIA

driving a *Vespa* up any ramp. I'm not flying through the air over six buses. Or even one. That's crazy. *Matto. Semplicemente matto.*[9] And you're not either, *piccolo signore!*"[10] She looked as if she might just whack Luigi. It was good for him that she couldn't reach him. "I ought to give you *un pugno,*[11] you little moron!" She sat back in her chair. And glared at Luigi.

Cincinnati—and everyone else—laughed at Luigi's guess and Luisa's reaction. Then the dancing pig got serious and looked straight at the two kittens. "Luigi, sometimes you go a little far. But, believe it or not, you're still on the right track."

Luisa looked startled.

Cincinnati unrolled the big paper and taped it to the wall. "I've made a crude poster. Maybe Poni will translate my words. Look at this," he said. And then stepped back out of the way so all in the room could read what was printed on the paper.

Big Show Tonight!

Free to All Birds and Cats

Daredevil Cats on Motorcycles

Amazing Tricks Never Before Seen

Tiny Orange Tabby Twins Run Wild on Vespas

BIG CATS ON MOTOGUZZIS IN DEATH-DEFYING LEAPS

Promptly at 7:00 p.m.

(Place goes here)

---

9. Crazy. Simply crazy.
10. little mister
11. a punch

Luisa gasped. "You're as crazy as Luigi, Cincinnati," she said. "I can't run wild on a *Vespa*. I won't run wild on a *Vespa*."

Buzzer Louis stood and smiled at the twins. "Not to worry Luisa. Do you really think I'd risk hurting you two? Just relax. It'll be okay. I promise. Let Cincinnati finish, please."

The dancing pig began again. "I'm happy we have everyone's attention now. Here's what will really happen. When some of Césare and the *tenente's* agents are catnapped, they'll be able to tell us where Fred-X and Frieda-K are taking the cats they're snatching. Then we'll plaster that town with these posters. Translated and made to look nice, of course.

"The posters are, shall we say, invitations. Special invitations. Invitations to Fred-X and Frieda-K to attend their own capture. How can they resist? So many cats expected in one place. With a special show by tiny orange tabbies— their favorites—running wild on *Vespas*. As Luigi might say, 'Santa Maria!' They're sure to show up early for front row seats.

"And when they do, we'll have a special surprise for them!

"Any questions?" Cincinnati knew there would be questions. A lot of questions. "Let's start with Dusty Louise."

"How are you going to pull off this little charade, Cincinnati?" Dusty asked. "You're not really going to turn those two little, little ..." she sputtered and pointed to the twins ... "little varmints loose on motor scooters, are you? And even if you do, how does that catch the two evil owls? I think I'm just as confused as ever."

Luigi spoke up. "Varmints? Varmints? Why do you call us varmints, Dusty? Just for that I'm not going to take you for a ride on my *Vespa*. No, ma'am. You can just walk!"

"Everybody calm down." Buzzer stood and gave Dusty and the twins a bit of a glare. "Maybe I'd better get to the end of this, Cincinnati. This question-and-answer session might not be a real good idea."

"I have some questions first, Buzzer." It was Césare. "If we know where the stolen cats are being held. And if we can attract Fred-X and Frieda-K to this show you are describing, then who will put on the show? Surely you don't propose that you and Cincinnati—and certainly not me or Poni—will actually do tricks on *Motoguzzis*. Do you? And how, and when, will we free the stolen cats?" He looked at Buzzer.

Luigi leaped onto the table and stood up tall. He turned to face Césare. "Patience, *cugino*," Luigi began. "We'll hire a band of roving gypsies to put on the show. And once the owls are caught, we'll all go break down the doors to free the stolen cats." Turning to Buzzer and holding both front paws straight out toward his big brother, he said, "Right, Buzzer?"

"Once again, Luigi, I can see that you're thinking. If everyone will just hold your questions, I'll tell you exactly what's going to happen."

He looked to Cincinnati. The dancing pig nodded as if to say, "Go ahead. Tell them before a fight breaks out. Right here in this room."

"No offense, Césare, but Cincinnati and I began working on this plan between our fuel stop in Gander and our arrival in Rome. We didn't know what we'd find when we got here. Except that Fred-X would be here.

"And if he's here, he's going to be stealing cats. It's what he does. Wherever he is.

"So we contacted Socks at Cats-in-Action headquarters. We

asked her to find—not a roving band of gypsies, Luigi, but a troupe of performers. Performers we had seen years ago in Antwerp. A troupe of Greek stunt cats. Cats who perform on motorcycles. They put on quite a show the night we first saw them."

"Where are they now, Buzzer?" Dusty just couldn't wait for the plot to unfold. As usual, she wanted the answer first. Sometimes even before she knew the question.

"Right this moment, Dusty, they should be arriving at the airport in Venice. In a C-130 transport plane. One kindly provided by our country's air force. To fly them and all their equipment from their gig last night in São Paulo. That's in Brazil, Luigi and Luisa."

"How will they know where to go?" Dusty, still impatient, wanted answers. And she wanted them now.

"They won't, Dusty. Until we tell them," Buzzer answered. "And we can't tell them until we know. And we won't know until some of our decoys are catnabbed and call to tell us where they're being held. Once we know the town, we'll notify the Greeks. And then we'll plaster that town with posters—spiffed up versions of the crude poster Cincinnati just showed you.

"The Greek stunt cats will head for that town, wherever it is. And they'll set up their big tent. And their ramps. And line up their buses. And do whatever else they do every time they get ready to do a show.

"There will only be one extra thing for them to prepare. And we'll help them do that. Now I know there are still questions you may have, but I see that French helicopter just got back. We need to move ourselves to the center of the action.

"We need to go to Moena." Buzzer meant to end the meeting and head for the helicopter. But Luigi and Luisa insisted on one more question.

"What?" Buzzer said as he looked at the little kittens.

"Ice cream!" the twins said together. "What about ice cream, Buzzer? You said 'shotguns, motorcycles, and ice cream. We got the shotgun part down. You're buying us *Vespas*, and those crazy Greek stunt cats will have the motorcycles. But you forgot ice cream."

"I didn't forget, you two. We just haven't gotten to that part yet," Buzzer smiled. "Now go get on that helicopter while I thank the airport manager here for lending us this room. And Cincinnati takes care of being sure *The Flying Pig Machine* can stay parked here for a day or two. As our grandfather Giacomo Spezzatino Giaccomazza would say, '*Andiamo avanti!*'"[12]

How do you suppose Buzzer, Cincinnati and their friends from Interpol will actually trap Fred-X and Frieda-K? Will the two giant catnabbing owls be fooled and actually go to the Greek stunt cats' big show? Is Buzzer really going to buy Luigi and Luisa *Vespas*? And let them ride in the show? And who's paying for all this, anyway?

---

12. "Let's go. Straight ahead!"

Impariamo un po' d'Italiano.

By Luisa Manicotti Giaccomazza

In everyday speaking you may wish to know how to respond to those speaking Italian. Here are a few words and phrases to help you get through many discussions.

In English	In Italian	Say It Like This
Thank you	grazie	GRAHT-zee-eh
You're welcome	di niente	dee NYIHN-teh
Hello	ciao	chow
Goodbye	arrivederci, or ciao	ah-ree-veh-DARE-chee, chow
Good	buono, bene	BWOHN-oh, BAY-neh
Very good	molto bene	MOHL-toh BAY-neh
Please	per favore	pear fah-VOHR-eh
At your service	ai vostri ordini	eye VOH-streh OAR-dee-nee
I want to introduce you	le presento	lay preh-SEN-toh
Sir	signore	seen-YOHR-eh
Ma'am	signora	seen-YOHR-ah
Miss	signorina	seen-yohr-EE-nah
What time is it?	Che ora é?	kay OHR-ah ay
Where are you going?	Dove va?	Doh-VAY vah
Ready?	Pronto?	PROAN-toh
Let's go	andiamo	ahn-dee-AH-moh
Okay/good	bene	BAY-neh
Sure	certo	CHAIR-toh
More slowly	piu lento	pew LEHN-toh
How's it going?	come va?	COH-meh vah
Maybe	forse	FOR-seh

Part Four

Gelato at the End of the Tunnel

"Owls smell funny! Cats rock!"

—Luisa Manicotti Giaccomazza

"I want to go to Venice. I want some
ice cream. And where's my Vespa?"

—Luigi Panettone Giaccomazza

* Chapter 14 *
A Gathering of Gatti

An Old Church in a Town North of Venice

The door to an abandoned bell tower at a very old church high on a hill creaked open slightly to the sound of rusty hinges. A shadowy figure in flowing robes crept in. He slammed the door shut. And the inside of the tower returned to complete darkness. A cat "meowed."

"Are you here my fine feathered friends?" the figure whispered. "It is I. Your protector from the Holy City. Umberto Uccello. The cardinal who saved you yesterday in the Vatican. If you're here, please speak to me. We have business to attend to."

"Up here. On the first landing, cardinal. But don't come up the stairs. We can talk from where we are. You might step on a cat. There are many here already. We have little time. And lots more cats to catch before there'll be enough to fill the first boatload. What do you want with us, cardinal?" The voice from above was that of Fred-X, evil catnabbing owl.

"I want to conclude our arrangement," cardinal Uccello said. "The terms. We must agree on the terms."

"We've already set the terms, cardinal. One-third for Frieda-K. One-third for me. And one-third for you. There's nothing to discuss," Fred-X responded.

"But I'm taking much risk, Fred-X," the cardinal pleaded. "And I have my two assistants to consider. Dominus and Vobiscum, the two crows from the radio station at the Vatican. They're demanding a cut."

"So give them a cut from your third, cardinal," Fred-X said. "We never invited them into our deal. It was to have been just the three of us. As usual, you're getting greedy. And we're doing all the work. You only have to lie to the Pope now and then, no?"

"Greedy?" the cardinal protested. "It is I who have offered you safe haven from the authorities. At any time. Day or night. You may come to the Vatican and escape capture. You know that. Is that not worth a bit more? How about one-half for my crow friends and me? One-half for you and Frieda-K?" The cardinal wanted to bargain.

"No. Absolutely not. That's our final word. Now get out of here before we decide to deliver a secret message to the captain of the Swiss Guard at the Vatican. And put a screeching halt to your career, you little swindler. I think they're already onto you, anyway."

"Or maybe we'll swoop down and scratch out your beady little eyes, cardinal." Frieda-K spoke. She was ready for violence. "The very idea of him wanting more!" she whispered to Fred-X. "He's lucky to get anything."

"Out of here!" Fred-X shrieked. "Back to Rome with you. Wait there for your money from the boat's captain. We don't want to see you again. Ever! Is that clear?"

The two owls watched from above as the cardinal slipped out the door to a big Mercedes limousine that waited for him. Cardinal Uccello looked out the back window of the car and up at the bell tower. "You will bargain with the cardinal, my feathered friends, before you're through. Or you will rot in jail. Forever." He smiled a wicked smile. And cackled the hideous laugh of a madman as his car pulled away, headed for the *autostrada*[1] and the security of the Vatican.

"Take me first to the wharfs in Venice," he said to the driver of his limo. He thought to himself, "I'll talk directly to the captain of this ship—this cat slave trader. He'll see things my way. Or I'll threaten to sink his ship." The cardinal cackled again. He was truly mad. *Pazzo!*[2]

* * *

In the Municipio di Moena

The owl-catching brain trust had barely set up shop in a borrowed room at the *municipio di Moena* when another report came in: two more cats missing. This time from nearby Passo San Pellegrino. Both were yellow tabbies. They kept the mice out of the *Albergo Costa Bella.*[3]

"*Allora*, at least we know they're still in the area," Césare said with some satisfaction. "And we've still got them surrounded."

Buzzer looked at Cincinnati and smiled. The dancing pig smiled back. "Césare's still thinking like a policeman, not a criminal. And certainly not like the evil Fred-X," Cincinnati

---

1. freeway
2. crazy, nuts
3. Hotel Pretty Hillside

whispered to Buzzer. "I don't think he gets what we're trying to tell him. But soon enough he'll see for himself."

It was late in the day and getting dark quickly. Sunset comes early when mountains surround you. *Signor Mano di Legno* finally understood who these cats and this pig were. And what they were doing. He wanted to help. He missed his two little yellow tabbies already. And he wanted them back. Safe and sound.

The *tenente* had been on a phone call for several minutes. She was nodding and taking notes. And now she was smiling. "*Sí, sí, capitano,*"[4] she spoke into the phone. "*Bene. Molto bene. Mille grazie, signore!*"[5]

Poni closed her cell phone and looked around the room to be sure everyone was present. "Listen to this," she said, calling the little group to attention. All eyes turned to her. And the room got quiet.

"I've just been talking with the captain of the Swiss Guard at the Vatican," she began. "You'll remember that they've been watching that cardinal who talked *il Papa* into giving safe passage to Fred-X and Frieda-K. And getting them a special and secret ride to the *stazione*. *Allora*, listen to this. The cardinal—his name is Uccello, Umberto Uccello—this morning he left the Holy City in one of their big black Mercedes limousines. He told his housekeeper he was going to the *alimentari*.[6] The *capitano* knows that's a lie. For two reasons: first, cardinals do not go to grocery stores; housekeepers do that. And second, even if he did go himself, he would never take one of the big

---

4. "Yes, yes, captain."
5. "Good. Very good. A thousand thanks, sir!"
6. grocery store

limousines on a short trip into Rome. The streets are too narrow and crowded for such a big *macchina*[7]. No, he would surely have taken a small *cinquecento*."[8]

"How long was he gone, *tenente*? And did the captain have him followed?" Césare wanted to know.

Cincinnati spoke up. "Let me guess, Poni. He's still not back. And the agent who followed the big limo on a *Vespa* lost it on the *autostrada*. The big limo hit two hundred kilometers per hour and left the scooter far behind. That about right?" the dancing pig asked, grinning.

Poni was stunned. "How do you know these things, Cincinnati?" she asked.

"Remember, *tenente*, Buzzer and I have done the work before that the Swiss Guard should have been doing. We know their traits. And we know what to expect from all kinds of shady birds. Including your Cardinal Umberto Uccello. It's just a matter of having been there. And done that."

"You are, of course, exactly right, Cincinnati. The cardinal has been gone all day and has still not returned. The trailing agent lost the limo the minute they hit the *autostrada*. I've asked the *capitano* to have someone call me the minute *signor* Uccello and his big Mercedes limo return to the Vatican.

"Meantime, though, Buzzer and Cincinnati, listen to this! The captain says he has two spies at the Vatican radio station. A couple of crows who are trying to get close to cardinal Uccello. The cardinal's asked them to help him get a larger 'donation' from some wealthy parishioners in the north of Italy. Uccello told Dominus and Vobiscum—those are the

_____
7. car
8. five hundred, a tiny Fiat

crows' cover names—he was sure he could get more money from these two 'rich birds,' as he called them. If they would help him. What does that sound like to you?"

Luigi spoke up. "I don't know what else it sounds like, but those crows' cover names are *pazzo*. Gimme a break! Dominus and Vobiscum? That's got to be a bad joke! Our kindergarten teacher, Sister Mary Cannonball, wouldn't like those names. No sir! No gold stars for those two crows!"

He folded his arms and stuck out his chin. Luigi had spoken.

Buzzer smiled. "You're right, Luigi. The names are lame. We can only hope that cardinal's elevator really doesn't go all the way to the top. But *tenente*, to answer your question, I'm now dead sure that birds of a feather are flocking together. That cardinal is somehow working with or helping Fred-X and Frieda-K. Bet on it."

Just as Buzzer finished talking, Césare's cell phone began to ring. He answered it.

"*Pronto. Qui il direttore Césare Pepperoni Giaccomazza. Parla, per favore.*"[9]

Césare suddenly sat upright. Then he stood and started pacing. "*Sí?*" he said, waving one arm in the air. "*Sí, Paolo. Buon lavoro, amico. Abbiatevi cura!*"[10]

He put down the phone and turned toward the group watching him. "We have a location!" he almost shouted. "That was Paolo. He and Guglielmo were snapped up about an hour ago. Fred-X and Frieda-K flew them to an abandoned bell tower at the church of Santa Vittore in a town called Feltre.

9. "Hello, ready. Director Césare Pepperoni Giaccomazza here. Speak, please."
10. "Yes, Paul. Good work, friend. Take care of yourself!"

It's about seventy kilometers north of Venice. They're locked up with two dozen cats so far. Paolo said the big owls just threw a priest—a cardinal—out of the bell tower. Then they left to steal more cats."

"Crank up that French helicopter, Cincinnati." Buzzer Louis was back in charge. "All of you, get into that helicopter right away. Dusty Louise, will you call the Greek stunt cat team in Venice? Tell them that 'location A' is Feltre. Ask them to get rolling at once. We'll meet them just north of the city. At a place that's called Pedavena on this map. Tell them to meet us at the big Heineken brewery there. They should be able to get there in less than three hours, even with their buses and big trucks. It looks pretty close to Venice."

Dusty almost burst with pride. She grabbed Buzzer's phone and started punching in the number he'd given her.

Expecting their question, Buzzer turned to the twins. "Feltre is about half way between where we are here in Moena and where you want to go, Luigi—Venice."

"At least we're still heading in the right direction, *mio generale*."[11] Luigi saluted. "Is there ice cream there?"

Will our owl catchers get to Feltre in time to turn all the cats in the bell tower loose? Who will take them back to their homes? What about Fred-X and Frieda-K? How many cats will they have to steal to make a full load on the slave trader's ship? And what will the ship's captain do if Cardinal Uccello threatens him? What about ice cream? How will Buzzer and Cincinnati get ice cream into plan B to capture Fred-X and Frieda-K?

------

11. my general

Impariamo un po' d'Italiano.

By Luisa Manicotti Giaccomazza

We have been visiting a lot of different towns in Italy. Maybe you would like to know how to pronounce their names.

Town's Name Is	Say It Like This
Roma	ROH-mah
Firenze	fear-EN-zeh
Verona	vair-OH-nah
Trento	TREN-toh
Bolzano	bohl-ZAH-noh
Moena	moh-EN-ah
Canazei	cah-nah-SZAY
Cortina d'Ampezzo	cor-TEE-nah dahm-PET-zoh
Predazzo	pray-DAHT-zoh
San Martino di Castrozza	sahn mahr-TEE-noh dee cahs-TROHS-zah
Passo San Pellegrino	PAH-soh sahn pehl-leh-GREE-noh
Venezia	ven-ETZ-zia
Feltre	FELL-tray
Pedavena	ped-ah-VEN-ah
Monte Belluno	MOHN-teh bayl-LOO-noh

* Chapter 15 *
Baiting the Trap

Feltre—In the Belluno Province, North of Venice

The night had been short for the owl-catching team from Interpol and the CIA. Buzzer told Dusty and the twins to "sleep fast" because they wouldn't be able to sleep very long. And he'd been right. They'd only been away from home two days. It seemed longer. A lot longer.

After meeting the evening before with the Greek stunt cats over *panini*[1] in the gift-shop *ristorante*[2] at the big Heineken brewery in Pedavena, Césare had tracked down a local printer. Citing a vague "international crisis," the head of Interpol from Rome had persuaded the printer to open up his shop. And to produce a hundred of Cincinnati's posters overnight.

Tenente Poni had met with the chief of the local *polizia*. Without telling him exactly what Interpol was up to—and never once mentioning CIA—she got him to find her the right

---

1. sandwiches
2. restaurant—usually bigger than a *trattoria*

official to issue permits. A permit to put up a big tent. One to put on a big show. And, equally important this morning, one to tack a hundred posters onto telephone and electric poles around the city. She had to promise that her associates would take them all down. As soon as the show was over.

Luigi and Luisa were getting bored. They'd had their breakfast and washed their faces. Even brushed their teeth. Everybody else was busy. Very busy. The twins were tired of sitting and watching. And full of energy.

Throughout the night, occasional hushed phone calls came in from Paolo and Guglielmo, the first two Interpol cat agents to be grabbed off and locked up by Fred-X and Frieda-K. They reported on the growing number of cats the big owls were bringing in. By early in the morning, there were more than eighty. And their numbers multiplied. Seems every few minutes, the two evil owls brought in another pair.

During the night, Fred-X and Frieda-K had snatched up the other six Interpol decoys. Every last one of them. So now all eight cat agents were among those locked in the abandoned bell tower. Every time Fred-X and Frieda-K left to get more cats, the Interpol *esche*[3] would tell the latest newcomers not to worry. "You'll all be free in a matter of hours. But don't speak to the evil owls."

Dusty wandered up to where Luigi and Luisa were staring out the window of the bed and breakfast where they had "slept fast" last night. Their host Alberto, a funny man recently returned to Italy from Australia, had made the little twins his special recipe of American scrambled eggs for break-

---

3. decoys

fast. And he was clearing away the dirty dishes. Tidying up the little dining room.

"What're you two doing?" Dusty asked.

Luigi just looked at her. He stared, in fact. Luisa said nothing, but watched to see what Luigi would say.

"Well?" Dusty wanted an answer. As usual.

Luigi looked at Luisa. Gave her his special look. It meant he wanted her to agree with whatever he was about to say.

"We're protecting the city from a herd of rampaging elephants, Dusty Louise." Luigi looked to Luisa, who nodded solemnly. "Remember that Hannibal guy the *tenente* told us about? Well, some of his elephants escaped. They've been living in the mountains. In caves. They've gone bad. And now they want to trample this entire town. What's the name of this place, Luisa?"

"Feltre." Luisa answered, trying not to snicker.

"Right. Those rogue elephants want to trample Feltre. But we've stopped them dead in their tracks. Sent them scurrying back to the mountains. To their caves. They won't be giving Feltre any more trouble for a long, long time.

"That's what we've been doing, Dusty. What've you been doing? Curling your eyelashes?" Luigi burst into laughter. Luisa lost her straight face and laughed with him.

"Very funny, you two. I guess I have to admit you've done a great job, though. I took a long walk after breakfast. And I didn't see a single elephant. Good work!" Dusty said with a straight face.

Luigi's face fell. It was no fun if you couldn't make Dusty puff out her cheeks. And make her eyes twitch. She must be getting over her snit about *Tenente* Poni. A good sign.

"Where's Buzzer Louis?" Luisa asked her big sister.

"He's gone to get you two a big, big surprise." Dusty smiled. Mysteriously. "You're going to be excited. Very excited, I'll bet." She just looked at the twins. With no particular expression on her face.

"Tell us, Dusty. What's the surprise? Pleeez!" Luigi wanted to know. But he and Luisa would never beg. Never beg Dusty, that is.

"See for yourself," Dusty said. "Look out the window."

"*Vespas.* Look, Luisa! Buzzer's got two *Vespas!*"

Sure enough, Buzzer and Césare had pulled into the little parking lot driving a tiny, three-wheeled *camioncino.*[4] Luigi and Luisa had seen the little trucks everywhere. They were called *ape.*[5] Little three-wheeled pickups. In the back of the one Buzzer was driving were two shiny *Vespas.* A big bundle of papers the twins guessed must be the new posters announcing the really big show tonight. And a little brown paper bag whose contents might be almost anything.

"Maybe there's *gelato*[6] in that paper bag, Luisa," Luigi said. "That would be perfect. *Vespas* and ice cream. Yes!"

I miei gemelli[7] scrambled through the open window and ran across the parking lot. Dusty joined them. But she walked casually through the door.

"*Vespas* for Luisa and me," Luigi yelled. "*Grazie, fratello mio. Mille grazie.*"[8]

"You take the *Vespa gialla,*[9] Luigi. "I'll take *rossa,*"[10] Luisa shouted. "We'll drive like crazy all over the place!"

---

4. pickup
5. bees
6. ice cream
7. The kitten twins
8. "Thank you, my brother. A thousand thanks."
9. yellow Vespa
10. red

Buzzer laughed. "Yes, the *Vespas* are for you to use today. And this *ape* is for Dusty Louise to use. But there'll be no 'driving like crazy all over the place,' Luisa. Besides, you said you wouldn't do that. Remember? You—all three of you—have important jobs to do to help us capture Fred-X and Frieda-K tonight. These *veicoli*[11] are tools to help you do your jobs."

"What's in the sack, Buzzer," Luigi asked. "It's ice cream, right? *Gelato al cioccolato.*"[12]

"No, Luigi. It's not ice cream. It's a little staple gun to help you do your jobs. But I promise you this. If you get your jobs done by early afternoon, we'll walk across the street to that store. See it? It's a *gelateria.*[13] They'll have dozens of flavors. And you and Luisa and Dusty can have any flavor you want. But first, you have important work to do."

"Work first. Then eat *gelato.*" Luigi saluted and hopped up onto the back of the ape. "What's our job, Buzzer?" Luigi asked.

"Let me guess," Luisa spoke up. "We get to staple all those posters up. All around town. Right? But what's Dusty Louise going to do?"

"Dusty's going to drive the *ape* slowly, very slowly, from telephone pole to telephone pole on the south side of town. You two are going to follow her on the *Vespas*. Every time she points to a pole, one of you is going to staple one of these posters to it. We want you to stay on the south side. The side closest to the church—Santa Vittore—where all the cats are being held in the bell tower. Most of all, we want Fred-X and Frieda-K to see these posters. To see a bunch of them.

---

11. vehicles
12. chocolate ice cream
13. ice cream store

"Do you all three understand your jobs?" Césare asked. He'd been quiet. Just watching. He and Buzzer had argued about having the twins and Dusty do this job. Césare thought it was too important to trust to "a couple of little scamps and a pouty spoiled brat."

Buzzer had held fast. "They may look like a couple of little scamps and a pouty spoiled brat to you, Césare. But they've proven themselves to me. Two weeks ago in Mexico, Dusty did a great job as our interpreter. And she's learning to fly Cincinnati's airplane. Luisa and Luigi cut off all their hair to make fake kittens out of a couple of gourds. Then the two of them actually stood right up to Fred-X just before we cuffed him. I trust them. Completely. They're all *investigatori più abile*,[14] my friend."

"*Sí. Capiamo*,[15] Césare. *Non ti preoccupare*."[16] Luisa assured her cousin.

"*Non dementicarti*,[17] Césare," Luigi added, looking serious. "We are all Giaccomazzas. The best of the best from Italy. Remember, *cugino*, if there's an important job to do, trust it to a Giaccomazza. *Vero?*"[18]

So that was that. Luigi had made their case. Even better than Buzzer had.

"OK, guys. Get going. See if you can get all these posters up in three hours. Then come back here. *"Ricordi la gelateria*."[19] Buzzer was beginning to recall and use some of the Italian from his early childhood. Cats, except those in Italy, forget their birth language as they grow up.

---

14. most clever detectives
15. "Yes, we understand, Césare."
16. "Don't worry."
17. "Don't forget, Césare."
18. Right?
19. "Remember the ice cream store."

* * *

At the Vatican—Back in Rome

A dirty, mud-spattered black Mercedes limousine crept into a back entrance to the Vatican. Its driver was exhausted. And he thought the cardinal, that crazy Uccello in the back seat, had finally gone totally mad. *Assolutamente pazzo.*[20]

Cardinal Umberto Uccello had tracked down the captain of the slave trader ship docked in Venice. Found him in a bar. Passed out.

Pouring water on him and slapping him awake was probably not a good start. The cardinal wanted to try to get more money from the captain for the cats Fred-X and Frieda-K were stealing. But *il capitano*[21] wasn't happy to meet the cardinal.

Threatening him had done no good, either. This captain had no fear of the cardinal. Or any harm the priest might try to do him. He had, in fact, slashed at the cardinal with the hook that had replaced his left hand years before. Screamed at him and sent him scurrying away. Defeated. And with no more money than he had come with. Still only a one-third share.

Taking note of the returning Mercedes limo, two crows perched on the broadcast tower of the Vatican radio station flew silently and swiftly across the *piazza* to the headquarters of the Swiss Guard. Dominus and Vobiscum would report in. Uccello, that crazy bird, was back.

* * *

---

20. Absolutely nuts
21. the captain

* Baiting the Trap *

Pedavena—A Park Across the Road from the Heineken Brewery

Demos, the swarthy solid black cat, head of the Greek troupe of stunt cats, gave his final command. "Pull. Once again. Pull.

"Now we're ready. Everything is in place. Gas up the *Motoguzzis* and the *Vespas*. And then get a little rest. Tonight will be something else." Demos finished shouting to his crew of stunt cats. He turned to *Tenente* Poni. "Right, my pretty?" he said, grinning an ugly grin that showed rows of nasty-looking yellow teeth.

Poni shuddered. She couldn't help it. She'd been watching the Greeks line up the buses, the barrels, and the ramps. And put up the big blue-and-white striped tent—the "big top." Now they'd rigged the final trap for Fred-X and Frieda-K. It was time for her to leave. To go back to the bed and breakfast where Buzzer Louis and Césare were waiting her return.

She'd been gorgeous since she was a tiny kitten. So the *tenente* had become used to being looked at. Leered at, in fact. Mostly by old male cats losing their hair and their teeth. But this Demos was giving her the creeps. "Why do all Greeks think they're God's gift to women?" she wondered as she thanked the big Greek and made her way out of the tent.

* * *

Feltre—Gelateria Trentun Sapori[22]

"I'm happy you like the *gelato*, Luigi. But try not to lick the bowl." Buzzer smiled as Luigi, Luisa and Dusty Louise polished

---

22. Feltre—Thirty-one Flavors Ice Cream Store

off their ice cream. Big bowls each of three scoops on top of a sliced *banana*.[23]

"Is this the ice cream part of plan B?" Luigi asked Poni as she joined the group. "Or do you and Buzzer and Césare and Cincinnati have something else cooking?"

"No, Luigi, this is just ice cream. For you and your sisters for a job well done. Thanks to all three of you." Buzzer smiled. "We'll get back to the rest of plan B—the ice cream—before too much longer. Soon," he promised.

Even Césare had to admit he'd been wrong to doubt the little twins and Dusty. The three of them had stapled up a hundred posters in just over two hours. Posters announcing the really big show tonight. "Cats on Motorcycles. Kittens driving like madmen on *Vespas*. Big cats in death-defying leaps on *Motoguzzis*." Posters clustered on the south side of Feltre near the abandoned bell tower of *La Chiesa San Vittore*.[24] Posters where Fred-X and Frieda-K would be sure to see them.

As invitations.

To their capture.

Will the evil pair of owls see the posters? Will the two of them be able to resist the lure of so many cats in one place? Is Buzzer and Cincinnati's plan B really diabolical enough to catch the catnabbers? And what does ice cream have to do with this plan, anyway? Will Buzzer and Cincinnati ever tell? Will Luigi make it to Venice?

---

23. banana
24. Saint Victor's Church

Impariamo un po' d'Italiano.

By Luisa Manicotti Giaccomazza

Here's a recap of some useful words and phrases that you can use when you travel in Italy. Italians like it when foreigners try to speak their language. Even if they get it a little wrong.

In English	In Italian	Say It Like This
Hello/goodbye	ciao	chow
How are you?	Come sta?	COH-meh STAH?
What's your name?	Come si chiama?	COH-meh see kee-AH-mah?
My name's Luisa	Mi chiamo Luisa	mee kee-AH-moh loo-EE-sah
Thank you	grazie	GRAH-zee-eh
You're welcome	di niente	dee NYIN-teh
Good morning	buon mattino	BWOH mah-TEE-noh
Good day	buon giorno	BWOHN JOHR-noh
Good afternoon	buona sera	BWOHN-ah SAIR-ah
Good night	buona notte	BWOH-nah NOH-teh
Goodbye	arrivederci	ah-ree-veh-DARE-chee
What time is it?	Che ora è?	kay OHR-ah ay?
Please	per favore	pear fah-VOHR-eh
I don't speak Italian	Non parlo italiano	nohn PAHR-loh ee-tahl-ee-AH-noh
I'm hungry	ho fame	oh FAH-meh
Glad to meet you	piacere	pee-ah-CHAIR-eh

* Chapter 16 *
Really Big Show

Under the Big Top in Pedavena

Night had fallen. Bright lights lit the inside of the big blue and white tent and the parking lot next to it, in the park across from the Heineken brewery in Pedavena. A cheesy brass band played slightly off key. Hundreds of cats, dogs, birds, and humans made their way slowly inside to bleacher seats on both sides of a long dirt ring. Ramps flanked three buses set in the very center. And barrels were set for precision riding drills on both ends of the arena.

"There they are," Cincinnati pointed. The dancing pig, Buzzer, and his brother and sisters were standing in the shadows under one end of the bleachers. "Fred-X and Frieda-K," Cincinnati continued. "On the front row in the middle. There. On the other side. See them? I knew they wouldn't be able to resist."

The two giant owls sat hunched over, talking quietly to one another. Glancing side to side, their eyes took in the vast number of cats pouring into the tent. They almost seemed to lick their beaks at the prospect of filling a whole boat full of these cats to sell as slaves.

"How do we get them, Buzzer?" Luigi asked. "Is it time for ice cream yet?"

"Not yet, Luigi," Buzzer said. "First we have to free all the cats locked in that bell tower across town. And lock these two up. Once and for all."

Tenente Poni closed her cell phone and spoke. "The Swiss Guard has arrested Cardinal Uccello. He's in a cell. Being guarded around the clock. They have enough evidence on him, thanks to those two undercover crows, Dominus and Vobiscum, to send him away for a very long time.

"The captain said to tell you *il Papa*[1] is most embarrassed. I believe the word he used was 'repentant.' The Pope has asked what he may do to make up for his mistake in helping Fred-X and Frieda-K escape," Poni said.

Buzzer leaned down and whispered into her ear. She listened. Then smiled and said, "I'll see what I can do, Buzzer. If he meant what he said, the Pope may just be willing." With that, she dashed off into a corner, punched in a number on her phone and began to talk in hushed tones.

"Césare, what about all the cats in the bell tower?" Cincinnati asked. "Have you made arrangements for them?"

"Ah, yes," Césare answered, looking at his watch. "In exactly seven minutes, they'll be freed. Then Paolo and Guglielmo and the other six agents held captive with them know exactly what to do. We're ready. Plan B is just too, too clever."

---

1. the Pope

"Buzzer!" Luigi tugged at his big brother's shoulder. "You haven't told us everything. When and how are we going to capture Fred-X and Frieda-K?"

"OK," Buzzer answered. He squatted down, picked up a small stick and began to draw a diagram in the dirt for Luigi, Luisa, and Dusty. He spoke softly so only the four of them could hear. He stood once and pointed to the roof of the tent. In the center.

Suddenly they all stood up. "That's it? That's all there is to it, Buzzer?" Luisa smiled. "It's truly very clever. Luigi and I are ready. Right, *mio piccolo fratello? Pronto?*"[2] She looked at her twin.

Luigi did what Luigi often does. He stood tall and saluted. But this time he saluted Luisa. *"Pronta!"*[3] he said.

Luisa smiled and said, "Then let's get those *Vespas* cranked up, Luigi. We have work to do. In exactly," she glanced at her watch, "thirty-four and a half minutes."

At precisely nineteen hundred hours—7:00 P.M.—the Greek stunt cats began the big show. First up was the grand march. A parade of a dozen cats on *Motoguzzis*. They rode slowly at first, around and around the arena. Then, as the tempo of the music increased, they speeded up. Until within five minutes they were roaring around the arena faster and faster, crossing in figure-eights at each end. They wore top hats with sparkling fireworks on either side. With the spotlight dancing around the arena, it was quite a sight.

Dusty sat in a folding blue canvas director's chair. She had a pair of high-powered binoculars trained on Fred-X and

---

2. my little brother. Ready?
3. "Ready!"

Frieda-K. "I'll let you know right away if either of them makes a move," she said to Buzzer and Cincinnati.

"They won't. Until exactly 7:30," Cincinnati said. "That's when the bus from the bell tower gets here and Luigi and Luisa dangle the bait those two owls won't be able to resist."

As the show went on, Buzzer and Cincinnati watched the clock move slowly. Time seemed to them to be dragging toward the magic hour.

The stunt cats put their machines through one-after-another acts that thrilled the crowd and caused them to applaud and cheer. Demos, the big black leader of the troupe, leaped a giant *Motoguzzi* sixty feet through the air, coming down right through a flaming hoop. It landed gracefully, almost without a bounce, to the surprise and delight of the big crowd. Demos roared around the arena, blowing kisses to the crowd. He slid to a stop and slipped through a flap in the tent, ending up out of sight of the crowd. But right in front of Buzzer and Cincinnati.

"We're ready, *signori*,"[4] he said to Buzzer. "Has anything changed?"

"No, Demos. Just watch Luigi and Luisa. When they take off, get ready to make the drop. And start the chaos. We'll wrap up our business as though it were part of the show. Once we're outside the tent, you can go on with your big daredevil jump over the buses," Buzzer said.

Cincinnati, checking his watch, turned to Césare. "The bus with the cats is here. Secure all the entrances. And have Paolo and Guglielmo bring them all right here."

---

4. gentlemen

"They still haven't moved," Dusty squinted through the binoculars and reported.

The *tenente* slipped up to Buzzer and whispered, "He said yes. He'll be there." She looked as if she could hardly believe what she'd just said.

Buzzer nodded and grinned at Poni. "Luigi's going to get his ice cream. Right where he wants to eat it. With a huge surprise to boot," he told the *tenente*.

Césare pointed to his watch. It read 7:28. While two cats on big cycles were thrilling the crowd with acrobatic stunts, Luigi and Luisa crept up to the entrance to the arena next to Buzzer, Cincinnati, and Dusty. The *mici gemelli*[5] were riding their red and yellow *Vespas*. Each had on a glittering helmet and a long, flowing cape. They looked ... well, they looked funny. Trailing behind them were cats. Lots of cats. Dozens of cats. The cats freed from the abandoned bell tower. Led by Paolo and Guglielmo.

At precisely 7:30, the lights in the big tent went dim. Luigi and Luisa entered the arena on their little scooters from behind a flap in a corner. Luigi turned left. Luisa turned right. A spotlight shined on each of them as they rode slowly in opposite directions around the outside walls of the arena. A hush fell over the crowd. Here were the promised "kittens on *Vespas*."

Slowly the lights came up, revealing that behind each of them was a long line of cats. Marching two-by-two. Twenty-five pairs of cats followed Luigi slowly to the left. Twenty-five pairs followed Luisa slowly to the right. They continued to circle the arena slowly. From opposite directions.

---

5. kitten twins

"We've got movement!" Dusty Louise spoke to Buzzer and Cincinnati. "They're talking to each other and shifting around. Not gonna be sitting there much longer, I'll bet."

As Luigi and Luisa rode their *Vespas* around the edge of the arena, they ended up coming toward one another. And meeting. Right in front of Fred-X and Frieda-K. Slowly they stopped their Vespas. Luigi turned to the right, facing the center of the arena. And then he stopped again. Luisa turned to the left, right beside him. She stopped too. The tent was silent except for the soft purr of the two *Vespas*.

Then both little kittens stood up on their scooters' seats and turned to face the big owls. In perfect unison, shattering the silence, they shouted, "Hey you ugly *brutti gufi*,[6] we've got your cats!" Luisa swears she saw Luigi actually stick out his tongue.

With that, they jumped back on the seats and roared to the middle of the arena, right in front of the three buses. A hundred cats scrambled after them. When they got to the middle, they all turned and gave Fred-X and Frieda-K a noisy group razzberry.

"They're moving! Now! They're going after Luigi and Luisa!" Dusty Louise shouted to Buzzer and Cincinnati.

"Exactly." Cincinnati had a one-word answer.

Fred-X and Frieda-K had jumped from their seats onto the floor of the arena and raced toward the center. There Luigi and Luisa and their two *Vespas*—and a giant crowd of a hundred or more cats—waited for them.

Demos raised both front paws high over his head as he watched the big owls scramble across the dirt. Then, in one swift motion, he dropped both hands.

---

6. ugly owls

All the lights went out, plunging the tent into total darkness. There was a loud "thunk," like a timber dropping. Then another. Followed by the screeching and howling of angry cats. A bunch of angry cats.

Buzzer, Cincinnati, Dusty, Césare, and Poni flipped on night-vision goggles and raced into the arena. And the fray. "Find the twins and get them out of there," Cincinnati called to Dusty and Poni.

The audience sat in stunned silence, not quite sure what kind of an act they had just seen. The noise coming from the middle of the arena began to fade. Until there was again silence. Lights flashed back on. And there, where all the action had started not thirty seconds before, stood two lonely *Vespas*. Alone. And empty. Their little engines idling.

A yellow one. And a red one.

The band struck up a lively march and Demos again appeared on his big *Motoguzzi*. Ready to race up a ramp and jump over three buses. To the absolute delight of the crowd.

❋   ❋   ❋

Regional Prison—Monte Belluno—Between Feltre and Venice
"You two were *magnifici. Splendidi. Che coraggio!*"[7] Césare raved on about Luigi and Luisa's role in the capture of Fred-X and Frieda-K.

"We are Giaccomazzas, Césare," Luisa smiled at her Italian cousin. "Never doubt a Giaccomazza." She winked at her gray tabby cousin.

---

7. Magnificent. Splendid. What bravery!

The two evils owls now were safely locked in cells. Interpol had ordered 24-hour guards. And a medical team to check out what damage a hundred angry cats might have done to them. In the fifteen seconds between the time the big overhead net was dropped over them by the troupe of stunt cats and when it was pulled out of the arena by Demos' crew.

"There were a lot of feathers flying," Luigi had said with a smile. "And most of them weren't attached to owls any longer." He laughed.

Buzzer and Cincinnati left the paperwork of getting the two owls into jail to Interpol. After all, they both were retired. So they had no real standing in the world of law enforcement any longer. Césare, as usual, had asked *Tenente* Poni to take care of it.

Owls safely checked into jail, she came back into the attorneys' lounge where the rest of the owl-catching crew was relaxing. After a job well done. And waiting for her so they could all go have dinner. A late Italian dinner, for sure. She looked at Luigi and Luisa. "Are you two really excited about tomorrow?" she asked.

The two kittens were still excited about what had just happened tonight. But they didn't know what Poni was talking about. They looked at her with questions in their eyes.

"I don't know," Luisa said. "Should we be excited? Nobody's told us about tomorrow yet."

Luigi looked at the *tenente*. "After tonight, Poni, only two things could make me excited about tomorrow. One is ice cream. And the other is going to Venice," he said.

Poni answered, "Then start getting excited. Get very excited, Luigi."

Now that Fred-X and Frieda-K have been caught with Buzzer and Cincinnati's diabolical plan B, what do you think is going to happen tomorrow? Will Luigi get to Venice finally? Will Buzzer ever explain how ice cream is supposed to be part of plan B? And who do you think Poni was telling Buzzer would "be there" tomorrow? Are you still wondering who's paying for all this action?

---

1. highway

Impariamo un po' d'Italiano.

By Luigi Panettone Giaccomazza

Hello, there. Luigi here. Luisa said I could write one little Italian lesson for you. I've seen what she's written for you in the last fifteen lessons. It's good, sure. But she's left out the most important thing you have to know to be able to travel in Italy. To travel and really have a good time, that is. Know what it is? How to say all the flavors of gelati. Here are enough to keep you eating for at least two weeks. Mmmmm!

In English	In Italian	Say It Like This
Vanilla	vaniglia	vah-NEE-lyah
Chocolate	cioccolato	choh-coh-LAH-toh
Strawberry	fragola	FRAH-goh-lah
Peach	pesca	PES-cah
Banana	banana	bah-NAH-nah
Cherry	ciliegia	chee-lee-AY-jah
Pistachio	pistacchio	pees-TAH-key-oh
Raspberry	lampone	lahm-POH-neh
Hazelnut	nocciolino	noh-cho-LEE-noh
Caramel	caramel	car-ah-MEL
Peanut butter	burro di arachide	BOO-roh dee ah-rah-KEE-dee
Coffee	caffé	cah-FAY
Neapolitan	napoletano	nah-poh-leh-TAH-noh
Peppermint	menta peperina	MEN-tah peh-peh-REE-nah
Tutti-frutti	tutti-frutti	TOOT-tee FROOT-tee
Sardine*	sardina	sahr-DEE-nah

---

*Mostly only cats like this one.

* Chapter 17 *
Finalmente!
Gelato Benedetto a Venezia[1]

"And so, Dr. Buford and Bogart-BOGART," Buzzer spoke into the little satellite phone, "Fred-X and Frieda-K are locked up tight. With 24-hour guards from Interpol. They won't get away this time. Césare, Poni, and Paolo are going to return Fred-X to Mexico next week. Señora Kay Tal and Sargento Pablo García of the Mexican Federales are coming to get him. The five of them will see that the evil owl goes back to the Yucatán to face the music. Frieda-K will be tried in Italy. Probably Rome. Our jobs are done here. Almost," Buzzer said.

"I must say your and Cincinnati's plan B was most clever, Buzzer. Truly diabolical," Dr. Buford said. "Great work. Please tell the twins we're proud of them. But you said your work's 'almost over.' What's left to do? Where are you now? And when will you guys be heading home?"

---

1. Finally! Blessed Ice Cream in Venice

"We're in Venice," Buzzer answered. "Or as they call it here, *Venezia*. Césare and Poni are showing Luigi, Luisa, and Dusty around. Taking them to the old neighborhood of our grandfather, Giacomo Spezzatino Giaccomazza, *il marchese*.[2] We should be heading back to Bolzano to pick up *The Flying Pig Machine* later this afternoon. Cincinnati likes to fly at night—especially over water. So we'll leave for Gander this evening. I sort of promised the twins we could stop there for a little while. They have some notion there's a big amusement park there. With a giant roller coaster. A place where they say Mother Goose lives.

"Of course, they're confused. But we'll never hear the end of it until they see for themselves. So I guess we'll be home tomorrow evening."

"What work do you still have to do in Venice?" Bogart-BOGART asked.

"Well, it's not really what you would call 'work,' Bogart-BOGART," Buzzer answered. "Remember that plan B included shotguns, motorcycles, and ice cream?"

"Right. But you're finished. Without ice cream. What gives?" Bogart-BOGART asked.

"Ice cream is why we're not finished," Buzzer said. "Listen to this."

* * *

Piazza San Marco—Venezia[3]

"And so, *mici miei*,"[4] Césare was saying to Luigi and Luisa,

---

2. the marquis
3. St. Mark's Plaza—Venice

4. my kittens

"this is the palace where our *nonno*[5] Giaccomazza worked and led the city state of *Venezia*. The world calls it *Palazzo Doge*.[6] But every cat knows it's really *il palazzo dei gatti famosi*.[7] It's right next to St. Mark's cathedral and the grand *piazza San Marco*, overlooking the bay. Beautiful, no?"

"What's in there?" Luigi wanted to know.

Césare answered, "*Oggi, è un museo*.[8] There are many works of art from the Italian Renaissance hanging inside. And there are many secret passages. Passages known only to cats. You must come back someday. Come back for a week. And I will call on our *cugina* Irene Mozzarella Giaccomazza to show them to you. To take you through all of them. And across the famous 'bridge of sighs' to the prison behind the palace."

"But for today, our time is up. We must return to the middle of the *piazza* for the big *cerimonia*."[9] Poni reminded Césare of the time. "Buzzer and Cincinnati will be waiting for us, Césare. With you know who," Poni said mysteriously.

"What ceremony?" Luisa shouted.

"Ceremony with who?" Luigi shouted even louder.

"Whom, Luigi," Luisa corrected. "Ceremony with whom."

"Whatever, Luisa. I just want to know what's going on? And when we're going to find out about the ice cream? And get some more of it to eat? I want mine to be *burro di arachidi*.[10] What kind do you want?"

Luigi might have a one-track mind at times. But at least he's consistent. And persistent.

"You'll see soon enough. Come with me," Césare said. He

---

5. grandfather
6. Doge's Palace
7. palace of famous cats

8. "Today, it's a museum."
9. ceremony
10. peanut butter flavored

took one hand each of the little twins and led them back through thousands of noisy pigeons toward the center of the *piazza*. Scattering the pigeons along the way.

*   *   *

Nel Centro della Piazza

"Looks like everything's ready, Buzzer," Cincinnati said. "The cats from last night—every one of those catnabbed by Fred-X and Frieda-K—are sitting around the tables at the *café*. Paolo takes them all home tomorrow. Now we need *il Papa*. And Césare, the *tenente*, Dusty, and the twins." He looked at the platform workmen had just finished setting up in the middle of the plaza. "Looks like CNN is here and ready. And RAI—the Italian TV networks."

Just as Cincinnati finished talking to Buzzer, a roar went up from the crowd that was gathering. A big black speedboat had just come down the *Canal Grande*[11] and pulled to a stop at the seawall next to the *piazza*.

"Right on cue," Buzzer said to Cincinnati. "There's the advance Swiss Guard team. And the Pope, himself."

"And here come Césare and the gang," Cincinnati said. "Good. We'll get this over with on time and be on our way."

"That might depend on how much ice cream Luigi can eat, Cincinnati. He'll remember that poodle Francois du Monde from the sausage eating contest. He might just try to outdo that record." Buzzer chuckled.

Luigi rushed up to his big brother. "Wait'll we tell you what

---

11. Grand Canal—the "main street" of Venice

we saw today, Buzzy! Our *nonno* might have been a bigger hero than you. What's all this ruckus, anyway? Who's that funny guy with the stick and the pointy hat?" Luigi leaped from subject to subject. As only he can.

"That 'funny guy,' Luigi, is *il Papa*—the Pope, himself," Luisa said quickly. "What's he doing here? I hope he doesn't let Fred-X loose again."

Buzzer leaned down and spoke softly to the twins. "Mind your manners. The Pope felt very badly about being hoodwinked by that cockamamie story from Frieda-K and Fred-X. He asked to come here today to thank us, and especially you two, for being so quick to catch them again. And save the cats of Italy. So be nice."

"Very bad, Buzzer." Luisa smiled.

"What?" Buzzer was puzzled by her statement.

"The Pope felt very bad," she repeated.

"That's what I said, Luisa." Buzzer was not getting it.

"Never mind, *fratello*.[12] "What do you want us to do?" Luisa began to think she'd never win the battle of proper use of adverbs. Or indirect object pronouns. In English. Or Italian.

"Just stay between Cincinnati and me. With Dusty Louise. Smile and wave. And be very quiet when *il Papa* speaks. And, Luigi, pay attention to what he's saying. Okay?"

"*Sí, sí mio capo. Attenzione! Diligenza!*"[13] Luigi saluted Buzzer. Then turned and saluted the Pope.

Dusty Louise just covered her eyes with both paws. "That Luigi's going to make fools of us, for sure!" she thought to herself.

---

12. brother
13. "Yes, yes, my leader. Attention! Diligence!

Reading Dusty's mind, Luisa said to her sternly, *"Non ti pre-occupare, sorella mia. Luigi e un disinvolto!"*[14] She smiled. "Figure that one out, Miss Priss!" she thought to herself.

Led by one of the Swiss Guards, every one of the owl-catching team members from CIA and Interpol climbed the steps and took their places on either side of *il Papa*. On a big platform.

Cameras flashed. Network light bars lit up. Sound recorders rolled.

And the Pope began to speak.

"Today we are come to the historical and beautiful *Piazza San Marco a Venezia*," he began. "To honor not just the cats gathered here. Those who were catnabbed and locked away yesterday. But all the cats of Italy. And the world. Too often we overlook the many gifts given to all of us by them. As an example, *il marchese Giacomo Spezzatino Giaccomazza*, marquis

---

14. "Don't worry, sister. Luigi's a cool hand."

of Venice. *Signor Giaccomazza* was a *Garibaldino*. Without him, Italy might not be a country. And today, we honor his descendants—Buzzer Louis, Dusty Louise, and *i gemelli*[15] Luigi Panettone Giaccomazza and Luisa Manicotti Giaccomazza. Their Italian *cugino*, Césare Pepperoni Giaccomazza. And from Cats-in-Action, Cincinnati the dancing pig. From Interpol *in Roma*, *Tenente* Poinsettia Fiore DeVille. And all their Interpol team.

"I salute you for fighting *crimine*.[16] And winning.

"And now, I present to each of you honorary membership in the Swiss Guard and these medallions to tell everyone, everywhere, that you're members."

With that, each of the owl-catchers was handed a leather box. Inside was a silver medallion struck with the symbol of the Swiss Guard. The medallions hung suspended from a striped ribbon. With purple and gold stripes. Separated by a silver thread down the middle.

The crowd cheered. Cameras panned and zoomed in on Luigi and Luisa.

"And now, a very special reward. First, for all the cats here who were snatched up by the evil owls, a big party. An ice cream party. Eat all the ice cream you want. The accounts of the fallen Cardinal Uccello, the Vatican's own 'dirty bird,' will pay.

"And for the bravest work of all. For Luigi and Luisa Giaccomazza, *nipotini*[17] of the old hero, himself, I give to you …"

Luigi flashed a glance at Luisa. She was staring.

"… all the *gelato* you could ever want. A lifetime member-

15. the twins   17. grandchildren
16. crime

ship in the Vatican's own 'Gelato of the Month Club.' Good work, Luigi and Luisa. Eat as much as you want today. But do not make yourselves sick. When you arrive home tomorrow, more will be waiting for you.

"Once again, as we say from time to time, *grazie amici miei*,[18] and peace be unto you." He looked straight at Luisa. And smiled.

With that, the Pope left the platform, led by the Swiss Guard.

And Luigi and Luisa raced for a special spot at the sidewalk café where all the cats were already dipping into their bowls of delicious *gelato italiano*.[19]

As they sat down at a little round table reserved for the heroes of the day, Luigi spoke to the *cameriere* who would serve only them. "*Burro di arachidi*[20] for me. And my sister here will have *pesca*.[21] At least for the first round. Thank you. And please," he added. Just a little late. And a little backward.

18. thank you, my friends
19. Italian ice cream

20. peanut butter
21. peach

Luisa was startled. "That's not what I wanted. Why did you order peach for me, Luigi?" she asked.

"The Pope said so, Luisa. I heard him. I was paying attention. For once." Luigi protested his innocence.

"What?! He never said that," Luisa laughed. "What did he say, Luigi?"

"He looked right straight at you and said, 'Peach be unto you. I heard it!"

Luisa fell out of her chair. Laughing hysterically.

How much ice cream do you think Luigi and Luisa will eat at the party? And when they get home, will they get a new supply every month? Will they ever get to come back to Venice to go through the secret passages of the Palace of the Famous Cats? And what of Fred-X and Frieda-K? Will they spend a long time in jail? Without any ice cream at all?

Impariamo un po' d'Italiano.

By Luisa Manicotti Giaccomazza

If you were to visit in someone's home in Italy—perhaps a cugino—you would want to know what to call some things you might find there.

In English	In Italian	Say It Like This
Apartment	*appartamento*	ahp-par-ta-MEN-toh
Bathroom	*bagno*	BAHN-yoh
Bathtub	*vasca da bagno*	VAHS-cah dah BAHN-yoh
Bedroom	*camera*	CAH-mair-ah
Ceiling	*soffitto*	soh-FEET-toh
Door	*porta*	POHR-tah
Elevator	*ascensore*	ah-shin-SOAR-eh
Floor	*pavimento*	pah-veh-MIHN-toh
Garden	*giardino*	jar-DEE-noh
House	*casa*	CAH-sah
Kitchen	*cucina*	coo-CHEE-nah
Light	*luce*	LOO-cheh
Oven	*forno*	FOHR-noh
Refrigerator	*frigorifero*	free-goh-REE-fair-oh
Room	*stanza*	STAHN-zah
Rug	*tappeto*	tah-PET-toh
Shower	*doccia*	DOH-chah
Sink	*lavandino*	lah-vahn-DEE-noh
Soap	*sapone*	sah-POH-neh
Stairs	*scala*	SCAH-lah
Toilet	*gabinetto*	gah-bee-NET-toh
Towel	*asciugamano*	ah-shoo-gah-MAH-noh
Wall	*muro*	MOO-roh
Window	*finestra*	fee-NES-trah

Epilogue

No Rest
for the Weary

"As long as there are criminals ... and crime.
Evil deeds ... and evildoers ...
we must never rest.
Never!"

—Socks

* Epilogue *
No Rest for the Weary

In the Air—Over Ohio

"Well, Buzzy, were you ever surprised!" Luisa said triumphantly. She and Luigi, one on each of Buzzer's knees in the cabin of *The Flying Pig Machine,* smiled at their older brother like they were the cats who just ate the canary.

"Never doubt a Giaccomazza, Buzzy," Luigi said. "We told you there was an amusement park at Mother Goose Land. You didn't believe us, did you?"

"No, guys. I really didn't. But I'm glad I was wrong. Did you like the roller coaster, Luigi?" Buzzer asked.

"You bet. It was fun."

"This whole trip's been fun," Luisa added. "Great fun. But I'm really tired. And I want to sleep in my own bed tonight."

Luigi looked serious. "Thank you, Buzzer. For letting us stop and play. Even though Mother Goose wasn't home. And you didn't believe a word of what we were trying to tell you."

Luisa added, "Your reward for being such a nice big brother

is, we're going to tell you a story now. So sit back and relax. Listen to this amazing tale of *due bravi mici*."[1]

Luigi began. "Once upon a time, four days ago, the phone at a house in the hill country rang. His eyelids were heavy. He blinked and forced his eyes open. Staring.

Luisa picked up the story. "It was the cousin of two clever and funny and cute and very brave little kittens. Orange tabby twins. This cousin's name was Césare Pepperoni Giaccomazza. All the way in Rome. He needed some help from the world's best owl-catchers. You see, Buzzy, two very evil . . ."

Her voice trailed off. She had fallen asleep. Right next to Luigi. Who was also asleep.

"That would have been quite a tale, I'm sure," Buzzer thought to himself.

Cincinnati wandered back from the cockpit. "We'll be home in a couple of hours, Buzzer. At least back to your home. We just passed over mine. I'll rest up a day or so if that's OK with you. Then I'll head on home. Can't let the dance studios run themselves forever, you know."

Buzzer Louis's little satellite phone rang. He looked at the caller ID and then up at Cincinnati the dancing pig. "It's Socks. I guess she wants a final report on Fred-X and Frieda-K.

"Hello. Buzzer Louis here," he answered.

Buzzer listened for a moment. Then sat bolt upright, almost dumping the sleeping kittens onto the cabin floor. His eyes slammed wide open. "No! C'mon, Socks! You're just kidding, right?"

---

1. two brave kittens

He paused and listened. Cincinnati, sensing bad news, stood by quietly.

"OK," Buzzer said into the little phone. "We'll be home in a couple of hours. Have them leave their numbers on our answering machine. Or give them to Dr. Buford Lewis or his very smart brother Bogart-BOGART. We'll call them as soon as we get there.

"What was that?" Buzzer asked. "Oh, sure, the owls are done for. No problem. Right, Socks, I'll call you as soon as we've talked to them."

Buzzer turned to his friend the dancing pig. "Remember Carlos?"

"You mean Carlos the Puma?" Cincinnati answered.

"The very same, Cincinnati."

"We did him in years ago in Buenos Aires. At the infamous international wine tasting and tango contest," Cincinnati said.

"Well, our old friend Carlos the Puma has escaped. Tunneled his way out of that terrible prison way up the Amazon River in Brazil. Nobody's ever escaped from there before. And lived. Until now." Buzzer was having trouble believing what he'd just heard.

"Do they want us?" Cincinnati already knew the answer.

"Afraid so, *amico*. The Brazilian and Argentinean police have been trying to reach us all day. I told Socks we'll call them back when we get home to the hills."

Cincinnati the dancing pig just shook his head and turned to go back to the cockpit.

Buzzer Louis closed his eyes. "Better get some rest," he thought to himself. "Tomorrow may be busy. Very busy."

Fine

Mille Grazie

Dozens of people are involved in the production of a book like this one. Without their help along the way, I might still be trying to figure out how to get Luigi and Luisa to Italy. So, our storyteller—Dr. Buford Lewis, Ph.D.—and I want to thank these very helpful individuals, in no particular order.

To everyone at Sunbelt Media, Inc., publisher of this tome. To Virginia for a great cover; to Pat for typography and book design; to Kris and Tommy for producing the books and filling the orders; and to Helen Bryant, a great and easy to work with editor. *Grazie.*

To illustrator Jason Eckhardt of Little Compton, Rhode Island, who did a terrific job, once again, of giving the characters visual personality and bringing them to life on the pages.

To translator Silvia Konrad of Center Point, Texas, a native Romana transplanted to the Texas Hill Country. *Grazie, amica*—for suffering through my pidgin-Italian. And fixing it.

To the perceptive members of the reader panel who plowed through a rough manuscript and provided extremely helpful feedback:

Adult Manuscript Readers
    Jim Arnold, St. Petersburg, Florida
    Barbara Arnold, St. Petersburg, Florida
    Pamela Deutsch, Dallas, Texas
    Jim Haynes, Dallas, Texas
    Barbara Ivancich, Seattle, Washington
    Tom Overton, Houston, Texas
    Lee Sneath, Dallas, Texas
    Cynthia Voliva, San Diego, California
    Marion Woodfield, Seattle, Washington

To Teacher Readers
    Suzy Groff, Bandera, Texas
    Krista Errington, Bandera, Texas

To Student Readers from Bandera Middle School
    Joseph Cruz
    Megan Ingle
    Donald Kassai
    Shelbie Martin

Finally, to the many members of my wife Mary's family in Italy who opened their homes, shared their tables, their *vino*, time and knowledge with us, *Grazie, anche a voi*.

In Moena: *Zia* Amalia DeMatté and *cugini* Rossina, María, Mariano and Tommaso DeVille; *cugini* María DeMatté, Ancilla Daríz, and Silvia Prandi. And *signor* Mano di Legno, whose real name I do not know, but who really works at city hall, dresses like a Russian air force general, cares for cats, and has a wooden hand.

In Trento: *Cugina* Beppina della Torre.

In Canazei: *Cugina* Lina Pitscheider and Pierangelo

Pitscheider; *cugino* Beppe DaVarda and *i gemelli*, Dino and Titsiano DaVarda; *cugina* Adrianna Ploner.

In Feltre: *Cugino* Sante Comarella and María Comarella. *E tutti i cugini* from the Turrin, Beppiani, and Comarella *famiglie*.

In Bolzano: *signor dottore* Luigi (Gino) Vadagnini, son of real *anti-fascistas* and a long-time prisoner of war in Siberia, for teaching us three important things: It's OK to make up wild tales; it's OK to tell others (the whole world, in fact) wild tales; and it's especially important to believe those wild tales one's self. A special thanks to you, Gino.

To all of you and those I may have forgotten to thank, *"Mille grazie, amici."*

Any mistakes you may find are mine, and mine alone.

—George Arnold
Fredericksburg, Texas
2006

Glossary and Pronunciation Guide
Common Italian Words and Phrases

English	Italian	Say It Like This
A	un	oon
Absolutely	assolutamente	ah-soh-loo-tah-MEN-teh
Accurate, real	sincero	seen-CHAIR-oh
Adventures	avventure	ah-ven-TOOR-eh
Airport	aeroporto	ah-air-oh-POHR-toh
Airplane	aeroplano	ah-air-oh-PLAHN-oh
April	aprile	ah-PREE-leh
All	tutto	TOO-toh
Also, too	anche	AHN-kay
Ankle	caviglia	cah-VEE-lyah
Apartment	appartamento	ahp-par-tah-MEN-toh
Apple	mele	MEH-leh
Arm	braccio	BRAH-choh
At	a	ah
At your service	ai vostri ordini	eye VOH-stree OHR-dee-nee
Attention	attenzione	ah-ten-zee-OH-neh
Assistant	assistente	ah-sees-TEN-teh
August	agosto	ah-GOH-stoh
Aunt	zia	ZEE-ah

English	Italian	Say It Like This
Bacon	pancetta	pahn-CHET-tah
Banana	banana	bah-NAH-nah
Baseball	baseball	BAH-seh-bahl
Basketball	pallacanestro	pahl-lah-cah-NES-troh
Bathroom	bagno	BAHN-yoh
Bathtub	vasca da bagno	VAHS-cah dah BAH-nyo
Bean	fagiolo	fah-JOH-loh
Beans	fagioli	fah-JOH-lee
Bear	orso	OHR-soh
Bee	ape	AH-peh
Beef	manzo	MAHN-zoh
Belt	cintura	cheen-TOOR-ah
Big	grande	GRAHN-deh
Bicycle	bicicletta	bee-chee-CLAYT-tah
Bird	uccello	oo-CHEL-loh
Birds	uccelli	oo-CHEL-lee
Blessed	benedetto	ben-eh-DET-toh
Black	nero	NAIR-oh
Blouse	blusa	BLOO-sah
Blue	azzurro	ahs-ZOO-roh
Boat	barca	BAHR-cah
Bolzano	Bolzano	bohl-ZAH-noh
Boots	stivale	stee-VAH-leh
Bowl	tazza	TAHT-zah
Boy	ragazzo	rah-GAHT-zoh
Boys	ragazzi	rah-GAHT-zee
Brave	bravo	BRAH-voh
Bread	pane	PAH-neh
Breakfast	prima colazione	PREE-mah coh-laht-zee-OH-neh
Briefcase	cartella	car-TEL-lah
Brother	figlio	FEE-lyo
Bus	autobus	ah-OO-toh-boose
Business	negozio	nay-GOHT-zee-oh
But	ma	mah
Butter	burro	BOO-roh
Café	bar	BAHR

* Glossary and Pronunciation Guide *

English	Italian	Say It Like This
Cake	*torta*	TOHR-tah
Canal	*canale*	cah-NAH-leh
Canazei	*Canazei*	cah-nah-SZAY
Candy	*caramella*	cah-rah-MEL-lah
Cap	*berretto*	bear-RET-toh
Captain	*capitano*	cah-pee-TAHN-oh
Car	*macchina*	MOCK-ee-nah
Caramel	*caramel*	car-ah-MEL
Care	*cura*	COO-rah
Take care (of yourself)	*abbiatevi cura*	ah-bee-ah-TEV-ee COO-rah
Cat	*gatto*	GAH-toh
Cats	*gatti*	GAHT-tee
Ceiling	*soffitto*	soh-FEET-toh
Ceremony	*ceremonia*	chair-eh-MOH-nyah
Certainly	*certo*	CHAIR-toh
Chair	*sedia*	SAY-dya
Cheek	*guancia*	GWAHN-chah
Cheese	*formaggio*	fohr-MAH-joe
Cherry	*ciliegia*	chee-lee-AY-jah
Chicken	*pollo*	POH-loh
Chin	*mento*	MIN-toh
Chocolate	*cioccolato*	choh-coh-LAHT-oh
City	*città*	cheet-TAH
City hall	*municipio*	moo-nee-CHEE-pyo
Clever	*abile*	AH-bee-leh
Climate	*clima*	CLEE-mah
Clouds	*nuvole*	NOO-voh-leh
Coat	*soprabito*	so-PRAH-bee-toh
Coffee	*caffé*	cah-FAY
Cold	*freddo*	FRAY-doh
It's cold	*fa freddo*	fah FRAY-doh
Cookie	*biscotto*	bees-COAT-toh
Corn	*granturco*	grahn-TOOR-coh
Cortina d'Ampezzo	*Cortina d'Ampezzo*	cor-tee-nah dahm-PET-zoh
Cousin	*cugino, cugina*	coo-GEE-noh, nah
Cow	*mucca*	MOO-cah
Crazy	*matto, pazzo*	MAHT-toh, PAHT-zoh

English	Italian	Say It Like This
Crime	*delitto*	deh-LEET-toh
Cup	*tazza*	TAHT-zah
Curious, strange	*curioso*	coo-ree-OH-soh
Cycling	*ciclismo*	chee-CLEES-moh
Dance	*danza*	DAHN-zah
Dancer	*danzatore*	dahn-zah-TOHR-eh
Daughter	*figlia*	FEE-lyah
Day	*giorno*	JOHR-noh
December	*dicembre*	dee-CHIM-bray
Decoy	*esca*	ESS-cah
Deer	*cervo*	CHAIR-voh
Detective	*investigatore*	een-ves-tee-gah-TOH-reh
Dining room	*sala da pranzo*	SAH-lah dah PRAHN-zoh
Dinner	*pranzo*	PRAHN-zoh
Director, boss	*direttore*	dee-reht-TOH-reh
Dog	*cane*	CAH-neh
Donkey	*asino*	ah-SEE-noh
Door	*porto*	POHR-toh
Doubt	*dubbio*	DOO-byoh
I did it	*lo ho fatto io*	loh oh FAHT-toh EE-oh
Dress	*vestito*	ves-TEE-toh
Dry	*asciutto*	ah-SHOOT-toh
Eagle	*aquila*	ah-KWEE-lah
Eat	*mangia*	MAHN-jah
Egg	*uovo*	WHOA-voh
Eight	*otto*	OHT-toh
Elevator	*ascensore*	ah-shen-SOHR-eh
English	*inglese*	een-GLAZE-eh
Enormous	*smisurato*	smee-shoo-RAH-toh
Espresso	*espresso*	ess-PRES-soh
Exactly	*esattamente*	ee-saht-tah-MEHN-teh
Excuse me	*mi scusi*	mee SCOO-see
Face	*viso*	VEE-soh
Family	*famiglia*	fah-MEE-lyah
Famous	*famoso*	fah-MOH-soh

* Glossary and Pronunciation Guide *

English	Italian	Say It Like This
February	*febbraio*	fehb-BRY-oh
Feet	*piede*	pee-AY-deh
Feltre	*Feltre*	FEL-tray
Finally	*finalmente*	fee-nahl-MEN-teh
Fine (quality)	*squisito*	SKWEE-see-toh
Fingers	*dita*	DEE-tah
Finished	*finito*	fee-NEE-toh
First	*primo*	PREE-moh
Fishing	*pesca*	PES-cah
Five	*cinque*	CHEEN-kway
Flavor	*sapore*	sah-POHR-eh
Floor	*pavimento*	pah-vee-MIHN-toh
Florence	*Firenze*	fear-REN-zeh
Football	*pallone*	pah-LOH-neh
Fork	*forchetta*	fohr-KET-tah
Forget	*dimentica*	dee-MEN-tee-cah
Don't forget	*non dimenticare*	nohn dee-MEN-tee-cah-reh
Four	*quattro*	KWAHT-troh
Fox	*volpe*	VOHL-peh
Freeway	*autostrada*	aw-toh-STRAH-dah
French	*francese*	frahn-CHAY-seh
Friend	*amico*	ah-MEE-coh
Friends	*amici*	ah-MEE-chee
Friday	*venerdì*	ven-ehr-DEE
Fruit	*frutta*	FROOT-tah
Funny	*buffo*	BOO-foh
Funny person	*buffone*	boo-FOH-neh
Garden	*giardino*	jahr-DEE-noh
Gasoline	*benzina*	ben-ZEE-nah
General	*generale*	jen-air-AH-leh
Girl	*ragazza*	rah-GAHT-zah
Girls	*ragazze*	rah-GAHT-zeh
Glass	*bicchiere*	bee-kee-AIR-eh
Glove	*guanto*	GWAHN-toh
Go	*va*	vah
How's it going?	*Come va?*	COH-meh vah
Let's go	*andiamo*	ahn-dee-AHM-oh

English	Italian	Say It Like This
Where are we going?	Dove va?	DOH-vch vah
Goat	capra	CAH-prah
Gold	oro	OHR-oh
Good	buon, bene	BWOHN, BAY-neh
Very good	molto buono	MOHL-toh BWOHN-on
Goodbye	arrivederci	ah-ree-veh-DARE-chee
Goodbye	ciao	chow
Good afternoon	buon pomeriggio	BWOHN poh-meh-REEJ-jyo
Good day	buon giorno	BWOHN JOHR-noh
Good evening	buona sera	BWOH-nah SAIR-ah
Good morning	buon giorno	BWOH-nah JOHR-noh
Good night	buona notte	BWOH-nah NOTE-teh
Good to meet you	piacere	pee-ah-CHAIR-eh
Granddaughter (young)	nipotina	nee-poh-TEE-nah
Grandfather	nonno	NOH-noh
Grandmother	nonna	NOH-nah
Grandson (young)	nipotino	nee-poh-TEE-noh
Gray	grigio	GREE-joh
Green	verde	VAIR-deh
Grocery	alimentari	ah-lee-men-TAHR-ee
Gymnastics	ginnastica	geen-NAHS-tee-cah
Hail	grandine	grahn-DEE-neh
Hair	capelli	cah-PEL-lee
Ham	prosciutto	pro-SHOOT-toh
Hand	mano	MAH-noh
Hat	capello	cah-PEL-loh
Hazelnuts	noccioline	noh-choh-LEE-neh
Head	testa	TESS-tah
Helicopter	elicottero	ehl-ee-COHT-tair-oh
Hello	ciao	chow
Hello (to answer phone)	pronto	PROAN-toh
Here	qui	KWEE
Highway	autostrada	aw-toh-STRAH-dah
Hip	anca	AHN-cah
History	storia	STOHR-ee-ah

* Glossary and Pronunciation Guide *

English	Italian	Say It Like This
Hockey	hockey	OH-keh
Horse	cavallo	cah-VAHL-loh
House	casa	CAH-sah
Hot	caldo	CAHL-doh
It's hot	fa caldo	fah CAHL-doh
Hotel	albergo	ahl-BEAR-goh
How	come	coh-MAY
Hunger	fame	FAH-meh
Hungry	affamato	ahf-fah-MAH-toh
I'm hungry	ho fame	oh FAH-meh
Hurry	presto, subito	PRESS-toh, SOO-bee-toh
I	io	EE-yoh
Ice	ghiaccio	ghee-AH-choh
Ice cream	gelato	gee-LAH-toh
Ice cream store	gelateria	gee-lah-tair-EE-ah
Immediately, quickly	subito	SOO-bee-toh
In	in	een
Incognito	incognito	een-coh-NYEE-toh
Incredible	incredibile	een-cray-DEE-bee-leh
I Introduce	le presento	lay pray-SIN-toh
Jacket	giacca	JOCK-cah
January	gennaio	geh-NYE-yoh
Jelly	marmellata	mahr-mehl-LAHT-ah
July	luglio	LOO-lyo
June	giugnio	JOO-nyo
Kitchen	cucina	coo-CHEE-nah
Kitten	micio	MEE-choh
Kitten	gattino	gaht-TEE-noh
Kittens	mici	MEE-chee
Knife	coltello	coal-TEL-loh
Leader	capo	CAH-poh
Leather	cuoio	KWOY-yoh
Leg	gamba	GAHM-bah
Legs	gambe	GAHM-beh

English	Italian	Say It Like This
Let's go	andiamo	ahn-dee-AH-moh
Lieutenant	tenente	ten-EN-teh
Light	luce	LOO-cheh
Lightning	lampo	LAHM-poh
Like (as)	come	COH-meh
Like (to like)	piace	pee-AH-chee
I like	mi piace	mee pee-AH-chee
I like it a lot	mi piace molto	mee-pee-AH-chee MOHL-toh
Lion	leone	lay-OHN-neh
Lip	labbro	LAHB-broh
Little	piccolo	PEE-coh-loh
Ma'am	signora	seen-YOHR-ah
Magnificent	magnifico	mahg-NEE-fee-coh
Man	uomo	WHOA-moh
March	marzo	MAHR-zoh
May	maggio	MAH-joe
Maybe	forse	FOR-seh
Midnight	mezzanotte	metz-zah-NOH-teh
Milk	latte	LAH-teh
Minute	minuto	mee-NOO-toh
Minutes	minuti	mee-NOO-tee
Miss	signorina	seen-yohr-EEN-ah
Mister	signore	seen-YOHR-eh
Moena	Moena	moh-EN-ah
Monday	lunedi	loo-neh-DEE
Monkey	scimmia	SHIM-myah
Moon	luna	LOO-nah
Moonlight	chiaro di luna	key-AHR-oh dee LOO-nah
More, most	piú	PEW
Morning	mattina	mah-TEE-nah
Mother	mamma	MAHM-mah
Mountain	montagna	mohn-TAH-nyah
Mouth	bocca	BOKE-ah
Much, a lot	molto	MOHL-toh
My, mine	il mio, miei	eel MEE-oh, mee-AY-ee
Museum	museo	moo-SAY-oh

* Glossary and Pronunciation Guide *

English	*Italian*	Say It Like This
Napkin	*tovagliuolo*	toh-vah-LYOH-loh
Neck	*collo*	COHL-loh
Nephew	*nipote*	nee-POH-teh
Niece	*nipote*	nee-POH-teh
Nine	*nove*	NOH-veh
No	*non*	nohn
Noon	*mezzagiorno*	metz-zah-JOHR-noh
No problem	*non c'é problema*	nohn cheh pro-BLAME-ah
Nothing, none	*niente*	NYIHN-teh
It's nothing	*di niente*	dee NYIHN-teh
November	*novembre*	noh-VEHM-bray
Now	*allora*	ah-LORE-ah
Number	*numero*	NOO-mair-oh
October	*ottobre*	oht-TOH-bray
Of course	*certo*	CHAIR-toh
Oil	*olio*	OH-lyoh
One	*uno*	OO-noh
Orange (fruit)	*arancia*	ah-RAHN-chah
Orange (color)	*arancione*	ah-rahn-CHOH-neh
Orange soda	*aranciata*	ah-rahn-CHAH-tah
Our	*nostro*	NOH-stroh
Oven	*forno*	FOHR-noh
Owl	*gufo*	GOO-foh
Owls	*gufi*	GOO-fee
Pants	*pantaloni*	pahn-tah-LOH-nee
Parents	*genitori*	gin-eh-TOHR-ee
Parrot	*pappagallo*	pah-pah-GAHL-loh
Passo San Pellegrino	*Passo San Pellegrino*	PAHS-soh sahn pel-leh-GREE-noh
Pasta	*pasta*	PAH-stah
Path	*sentiero*	sehn-tee-AIR-oh
Peach	*pesca*	PESS-cah
Peanuts	*arachidi*	ah-rah-KEY-dee
Salted peanuts	*arichidi con sale*	ah-rah-KEY-dee cohn SAH-leh
Pear	*pera*	PAIR-ah

English	Italian	Say It Like This
Pedavena	Pedavena	ped-ah-VEN-ah
Pepper	pepe	PEH-peh
Peppermint	menta peperina	MEN-tah pep-peh-REE-nah
Pickup	camioncino	cah-mee-ohn-CHEE-noh
Pig	maiale	my-AH-leh
Pistachio	pistacchio	pees-TAH-key-oh
Pizza	pizza	PEETZ-zah
Plate	piatto	pee-AH-toh
Plaza	piazza	pee-AHT-zah
Please	per favore	pair fah-VOH-reh
Police	polizia	poh-leet-ZEE-ah
Policemen	poliziotto	poh-lee-zee-OH-toh
Pope	il Papa	eel PAH-pah
Potato	patata	pah-TAH-tah
Predazzo	Predazzo	pray-DAHT-zoh
Punch (to hit)	pugno	POO-nyoh
Quickly	velocemente	veh-loh-cheh-MEHN-teh
Question	domanda	doh-MAHN-dah
Rabbit	coniglio	coh-NEE-lyo
Rain	piove	pee-OH-veh
Rainy	piovoso	pee-oh-VOH-soh
It's raining	sta piovendo	stah pee-oh-VEHN-doh
Raincoat	impermeabile	eem-pear-meh-AH-bee-leh
Raspberry	lampone	lahm-POH-neh
Ready	pronto	PROHN-toh
Red	rosso	ROH-soh
Refrigerator	frigorifero	free-goh-REE-fair-oh
Remember	recorda	reh-COHR-dah
Restaurant	ristorante	ree-store-AHN-teh
Restaurant (small)	trattoria	trah-toh-REE-ah
Road	strada	STRAH-dah
Room	stanza	STAHN-zah
River	fiume	FYOO-meh
Rome	Roma	ROH-mah
Rug	tappeto	tahp-PET-oh
Running	corsa	COHR-sah

* Glossary and Pronunciation Guide *

English	Italian	Say It Like This
Sailing	navigare	nah-vee-GAH-reh
Salad	insalata	een-sah-LAH-tah
Salt	sale	SAH-leh
Sandwich	panino	pah-NEE-noh
Sandwiches	panini	pah-NEE-nee
San Martino di Castrozza	San Martino di Castrozza	sahn mar-TEE-no dee cahs-STOHS-zah
Saturday	sabato	SAH-bah-toh
Sausage	salsiccia	sahl-SEE-chah
Say	dica	DEE-cah
Say it	lo dica	loh DEE-cah
Scarf	sciarpa	SHAR-pah
Sea	mare	MAHR-eh
Second	secondo	say-COHN-doh
September	settembre	set-TEHM-bray
Sergeant	sergente	sair-GIN-teh
Seven	sette	SET-teh
Sheep	pecora	PECK-oh-rah
Ship	nave	NAH-veh
Shirt	camicia	cah-MEE-chah
Shoes	scarpe	SCAR-peh
Shoulder	spalla	SPAHL-lah
Shower	doccia	DOH-chah
Sidewalk	marciapiede	MAHR-chah pee-AID-ee
Sink	lavandino	lah-vahn-DEE-noh
Sir	signore	seen-YOHR-eh
Sister	sorella	soh-REL-lah
Six	sei	say
Skiing	corsa con gli sci	COHR-sah cohn lyee SHEE
Skirt	sottana	soat-TAH-nah
Skunk	puzzola	pootz-ZOH-lah
Sleuth	segugio	say-GOO-joe
Slowly	lentamente	lehn-tah-MEN-teh
More slowly	piú lentamente	pew lehn-tah-MEN-teh
Small	piccolo	PEEK-coh-loh
Snake	serpente	sair-PEN-teh
Snow	neve	NEH-veh
So	tanto	TAHN-toh

English	Italian	Say It Like This
Soap	sapone	sah-POH-neh
Soccer	calcio	CAHL-choh
Socks	calzine	cahl-ZEE-neh
Son	figlio	FEE-lyoh
I'm sorry	mi dispiace	mee deese-pee-AH-chee
Soup	zuppa	ZOO-pah
Speak	parla	PAHR-lah
Spoon	cucchiaio	coo-CHY-yoh
Squid	calamari	cah-lah-MAHR-ee
State police	carabinieri	cah-rah-bean-YAIR-eh
Station, railroad	stazione	statz-ee-OH-neh
Steps, stairs	scala	SCAH-lah
Stomach	stomaco	STOH-mah-coh
Storm	tempesta	tem-PESS-tah
Strange	curioso	coo-ree-OH-soh
Strawberries	fragole	FRAH-goh-leh
Straight ahead	diritto	dee-REET-toh
Stream	corrente	cohr-REN-teh
Street	via	VEE-ah
Suitcase (small)	valigetta	vah-lee-JET-tah
Suitcase (large)	valigia	vah-lee-jah
Sun	sole	SOH-leh
Sunlight	luce del sole	LOO-cheh del SOH-leh
Sunday	domenica	doh-MIN-ee-cah
Super	di prim 'ordine	dee preem OHR-dee-neh
Sure	sicuro	see-COO-roh
Surveyor	geometra	gee-oh-MET-rah
Sweater	maglione	mah-LYOH-neh
Swimming	nuoto	noo-OH-toh
Table	tavola	TAH-voh-lah
Tablecloth	tovaglia	toh-VAH-lya
Teeth	denti	DEN-tee
Telephone	telefono	teh-LAY-foh-noh
Temperature	temperatura	tem-pear-ah-TOOR-ah
Ten	dieci	dee-AY-chee
Tennis	tennis	TEN-nees
Thanks, thank you	grazie	GRAH-zee-eh

* Glossary and Pronunciation Guide *

English	Italian	Say It Like This
Thousand	mille	MEE-leh
Three	tre	tray
Thunder	tuono	too-OH-noh
Thursday	giovedi	joh-veh-DEE
Tiger	tigre	TEE-greh
Time	tempo	TEHM-poh
On time	in punto	een POON-toh
All the time	tutto il tempo	TOO-toh eel TEHM-poh
From time to time	di tanto in tanto	dee TAHM-toh een TAHN-toh
Next time	la prossima volta	lah PROS-see-mah VOHL-tah
What time is it?	Che ora é?	kay OH-rah AY
I'm tired	sono stanco	SOH-noh STAHN-coh
Today	oggi	OH-gee
Toe	dito del piede	DEE-toh del pee-AY-dee
Toilet	gabinetto	gah-bee-NET-toh
Tomato	pomodoro	poh-moh-DOHR-oh
Tomorrow	domani	doh-MAH-nee
Tongue	lingua	LEEN-gwah
Too, also	anche	AHN-kay
Me, too	anche io	AHN-kay EE-yoh
Towel	asciugamano	ah-shoo-gah-MAH-noh
Train	treno	TREHN-oh
Trent	Trento	TREN-toh
Truck	camion	cah-mee-OHN
Tuesday	martedi	mahr-teh-DEE
Turtle	tartaruga	tar-tah-ROO-gah
Twenty	venti	VAIN-tee
Twins	gemelli	jeh-MEL-lee
Two	due	DOO-eh
Umbrella	ombrello	ohm-BREL-loh
Unbelievable	incredibile	een-cray-DEE-bee-leh
Uncle	zio	ZEE-oh
Understand	capisce	cah-PEESH-eh
Underwear	biancheria intima	bee-ahn-care-EE-ah EEN-tee-mah
I understand	capisco	cah-PEESH-coh
I don't understand	non capisco	nohn cah-PEESH-coh

English	Italian	Say It Like This
United States	*Stati Uniti*	STAH-tee oo-NEE-tee
Vanilla	*vaniglia*	vah-NEE-lyah
Vehicles	*veicoli*	vay-EE-coh-lee
Venice	*venezia*	ven-ET-zia
Venison	*carne di cervo*	CAHR-neh dee CHAIR-voh
Volleyball	*palla a volo*	pah-lah ah VOH loh
Waiter	*cameriere*	cah-mair-eh-AIR-eh
Wall	*muro*	MOO-roh
Wasp	*vespa*	VEHS-pah
To watch, to observe	*osservare*	oss-air-VAHR-eh
Water	*acqua*	OCK-wah
Mineral water	*acqua minerale*	OCK-wah meen-air-AHL-eh
Weather	*tempo*	TEM-poh
Welcome	*benvenuto*	ben-veh-NOO-toh
You're welcome	*di niente*	dah NYIHN-teh
What	*quale*	KWAH-leh
When	*quando*	KWAHN-doh
Where	*dove*	DOH-veh
Who	*che*	kay
Who knows?	*Chi lo sa?*	key loh-SAH
Wednesday	*mercoledi*	mair-coh-leh-DEE
Well	*bene*	BAY-neh
Very well	*molto bene*	MOHL-toh BAY-neh
White	*bianco*	bee-AHN-coh
Wind	*vento*	VEN-toh
It's windy	*tira vento*	TEER-ah VEN-toh
Window	*finestra*	fee-NES-trah
Wine	*vino*	VEE-noh
Without	*senza*	SEHN-zah
Wolf	*lupo*	LOO-poh
Wood	*legno*	LAY-nyoh
Word	*parola*	pah-ROH-lah
Work	*lavoro*	lah-VOH-roh
Worried	*preoccupato*	pray-oh-coo-PAH-toh
Don't worry	*non ti preoccupare*	nohn tee pray-oh-coo-PAH-reh
Wrist	*polso*	POHL-soh

* Glossary and Pronunciation Guide *

English	Italian	Say It Like This
Yellow	giallo	JAHL-loh
Yes	sí	see
Zucchini	zucchini	zoo-KEY-nee

About the Authors

The Storyteller

Dr. Buford Lewis, Ph.D., also known as "The Hillbilly Literati," is the only known living canine (a Labrador retriever) to have earned a doctor of philosophy degree. Buford is professor *emeritus* and holds the Rin Tin Tin chair of literature at the University of California at Barkley. Before taking up residence in the Texas Hill Country, Dr. Lewis served as press secretary to a succession of governors of California.

The Author

Following a thirty-plus year career in advertising and public relations in Dallas, the last twenty-two as president and chief operating officer of one of the Southwest's more creative agencies, George retired to the Texas Hill Country where he and his wife of more than forty years raise coastal Bermuda hay, registered half-Arabian horses, dogs, cats, and invisible goats.

His first book in 2003, *Growing Up Simple: An Irreverent Look at Kids in the 1950s*, with foreword by Texas humorist Liz Carpenter, was an instant critical and sales success, winning international awards for humor, regional awards for writing and content, and a coveted Silver Spur.

In 2005's *Los Gatos of the CIA: Hunt for Fred-X*, he introduced the world to the characters in this book. Their first adventure, in Mexico at the invitation of *El Presidente* Vicente Fox, initiated the concept of learning foreign vocabulary—particularly for juvenile readers—in English context... a practice continued in *I Gatti of the CIA: Fred-X Rising* (2006).

Fred-X Rising is his fourth book from Sunbelt Media and his second fiction novel for juvenile readers and mystery and cat lovers of all ages.

Visit

www.CIAcats.com